ALSO BY RICHARD PAUL EVANS

The Sunflower
A Perfect Day
The Last Promise
The Christmas Box Miracle
The Carousel
The Looking Glass
The Locket
The Letter
Timepiece
The Christmas Box

For Children
The Dance
The Christmas Candle
The Spyglass
The Tower
The Light of Christmas

✴RICHARD PAUL EVANS✴

FINDING

Noel

DOUBLEDAY LARGE PRINT HOME LIBRARY EDITION

SIMON & SCHUSTER
NEW YORK   LONDON   TORONTO   SYDNEY

This Large Print Edition, prepared especially for Doubleday Large Print Home Library, contains the complete, unabridged text of the original Publisher's Edition.

SIMON & SCHUSTER
Rockefeller Center
1230 Avenue of the Americas
New York, NY 10020

SIMON & SCHUSTER and colophon are registered trademarks of Simon & Schuster, Inc.

Manufactured in the United States of America

ISBN-13: 978-0-7394-7493-8

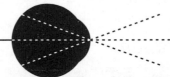

This Large Print Book carries the
Seal of Approval of N.A.V.H.

✳ A C K N O W L E D G M E N T S ✳

irst and foremost, *tante grazie* to my sweetheart, Keri, for being my home and heart.

I would like to thank the usual cast for their *unusual* patience and support during the difficult times I went through while writing this book: my agent Laurie Liss and my S&S friends: my editor Sydny Miner (thank you, Syd, for your empathy and reassurances), and my publishers David Rosenthal and Carolyn Reidy.

I'd like to thank my talented and insightful new writing assistant, Jenna Evans.

Also, thank you Gypsy da Silva, Emily Benton and Karen Roylance for your editorial assistance.

I'd like to say goodbye to my assistant Kelly Gay. It's been a pleasure working with you over the past few years. (Boomer too.)

While this book is wholly a work of fiction—

as are its characters—many of Macy's experiences in this book were inspired by the real life experiences of my dear friend Celeste Edmunds. I am grateful to Celeste for her assistance with my research but mostly for sharing with me the stories of her past and allowing me to recreate them in my book. For those who feel my character Macy is too resilient, good-hearted and untarnished by the atrocities of her past to be credible, I invite them to meet Celeste.

In memory of June Sue Carol Thorup Evans

My first published work was a tale I wrote in the first grade at Hugo Reid Elementary School in Arcadia, California. My story was called "The Blue Bunny," and it was printed in the school's annual creative works publication. My mother treated it as a masterpiece of American literature. From "The Blue Bunny" on, my mother was my biggest fan.

I lost my biggest fan on Valentine's Day of this year. This story is for her.

FINDING Noel

CHAPTER

One

Begin at the start, end at the end.
It's the best advice I could give a friend.

✦ SONG LYRICS FROM MARK SMART'S DIARY ✦

When I was a boy, my mother told me that everyone comes into our lives for a reason. I'm not sure if I believe that's true. The thought of God weaving millions of lives together into a grand human tapestry seems a bit fatalistic to me. Still, as I look back at my life, there seem to be times when such divinity is apparent. None is more obvious to me than that winter evening when I met a beautiful young woman named Macy and there ensued the extraordinary chain of events that encounter set in place.

Of course such a theory carried to the extreme would mean that God sabotaged my car that night because, had my car's timing belt not broken at that precise moment, this story never would have happened. But it did, and my life was forever changed. Perhaps my mother was right. If God can align the planets, maybe He can do the same to our lives.

✳

My story began at a time when it was dangerously close to ending—a wintry November evening, eleven days after my mother died. My mother was killed in a car accident. There were three other people with her in the car, and everyone but my mother walked away unharmed. I was close to my mother, and the day I learned she died was the worst day of my life.

Even before her death my life was in shambles. I had left my home in Huntsville, Alabama, nine months earlier and come to Salt Lake City to attend the University of Utah on an engineering scholarship. I had never been out West, and all I knew of Utah (other than that it had the only out-of-state school willing to give me a scholarship) was that it was a long way from Huntsville, with a few mountain ranges in between. This suited me because I wanted to put as many miles between my father and me as I could.

Actually, I never really called Stuart Smart "Father." He had always been "Stu" to me, and I considered his full name an oxymoron. He was an auto mechanic with an eighth-grade education, grease under his fingernails, and a disdain for all things he didn't understand—which included English grammar and me.

His dream was for me to one day take over the family business—Smart Auto Repair—and every Saturday after I turned ten, he'd drag me down to the garage and put me to work. While my friends were hanging around the Tastee-Freez or hunting grasshoppers with BB guns, I spent my childhood changing tires and air filters.

I hated everything about the garage; from the boredom of watching Stu dissect a transmission to eating bologna and mustard sandwiches on bread smudged with motor oil. But most of all I didn't like being with Stu. He wasn't one for idle conversation, so the long days were mostly silent except for the occasional whine of a pneumatic wrench and the constant twang of a country radio station. I wasn't much good as a mechanic and Stu always seemed annoyed with my ineptness. Every week I begged my mother to not make me go, and one Saturday, around the time I turned fourteen, Stu finally gave up on me and left me home.

*If love isn't blind it's at least
horribly nearsighted.*
—Mark Smart's Diary

My mother, Alice Geniel Phelps, was nothing like Stu. She was soft, well spoken and thoughtful. She liked to read and talk about philosophy, music and literature, things my father generally considered a waste of time. I could never figure out why someone like my mother married a guy like Stu until I came across a copy of my parents' wedding announcement. To my surprise I learned that they'd been married just eight weeks before I was born. I figured that with the way things were back then, she had to.

As I got older, Stu and I argued a lot. I couldn't tell you how many times my mother interceded on my behalf, sometimes standing between the two of us. My mother was the skin that held our home together. Now she was gone. And so was my home.

As I said, things were already going badly. Though I worked hard and earned straight A's, after my first year in school, the university announced a budgetary cutback and dropped hundreds of scholarships. Mine included. Since I was no longer in school, I lost my job at the university registrar's office and my room in the dorm.

In truth, I didn't care that much about engineering—I had no real love for it—but my parents couldn't afford tuition and the scholarship was my only way into college. My real dream was to be a songwriter. But music scholarships are hard to come by unless you're a classical virtuoso, which I'm not. I play the twelve-string guitar alright. I guess I'm more of a folksinger, not exactly Juilliard material.

Stu had predicted my failure and I wasn't about to give him the satisfaction of making him right, so I stayed in Utah and wrote cheerful, fraudulent letters home, telling everyone that school was going well. The truth was I was lonely, poor and depressed, living in a rundown basement apartment and employed at the only job I could find—on the janitorial crew at a nearby high school.

My plan was to save up enough money to get back into school, but I was barely making enough to get by. The day my mother died, my aunt called the dorm to tell me. That's when my family learned I was no

longer in school. Since I had left no forward-
ing address or phone number, I didn't find
out about my mother's death until two days
after her funeral when I called home to talk
to her. Stu answered the phone. He called
me a liar and told me not to bother to come
home.

I thought I'd hit bottom, but apparently
there was still more room to fall. Later that
same week Tennys, my girlfriend back in
Alabama, whom I had dated for nearly four
years, sent me a letter informing me of her
recent engagement to a promising young
chiropractor.

I'm ashamed of what happened next. I
now believe that under the right circumstances we are all capable of things we'd
never think possible.

In the last year I had struggled with depression. But now, with the added grief,
loneliness and rejection, I began having
thoughts of ending my life. At first it was no
more than an errant spark, quickly extinguished. But as my depression deepened,
the idea began to take root.

The night this story begins I had arrived
at work only to be yelled at by a crazy English teacher who accused me of stealing a

classroom CD player. I knew nothing of the player, had never even noticed it, but she insisted that I was the only one with access to her room and she swore I'd be fired and reported to the police if I didn't return it by the next day. Later that evening, as I cleaned toilets, I decided this would be my last night of pain. That was where my mind was when my car broke down on the way home from work. God kicking me one last time, I thought. The truth was He had other plans.

My mother used to say, "Man's extremities are God's opportunities." She also used to say, "Be kind to everyone—you don't know what cross they're bearing and how sweet that kind word might ring." That night proved both pieces of wisdom true.

That night was the start of a journey that taught me that one truth can change everything. It was the night I found Macy. And it was the Christmas season that Macy found Noel.

CHAPTER

Two

My mother used to tell me that angels walk the earth disguised as people. Tonight I'm a believer.

✦MARK SMART'S DIARY✦

NOVEMBER 3, 1988

"What the . . ."

My windshield wipers swung wildly in a vain attempt to clear the snow from my windshield, as my sixteen-year-old Malibu coughed, shuddered, then stalled, the dashboard lighting up like a Christmas tree. It was almost midnight and Salt Lake was in the clutch of an early snowfall. A blizzard, actually. I had just finished work and was headed home on snow-packed roads, wondering if I was really capable of ending my life. Considering the direction my thoughts were taking, it seems peculiar that my car breaking down bothered me. But it did. *Just another sign of God's boundless love,* I thought cynically.

I coasted the Malibu to the side of the road, bumping into the snow-covered curb. I punched the steering wheel in frustration. For all the time I spent in Stu's shop, I knew relatively little about cars. Stu would've known what was wrong before I came to a stop. I saw a movie once about a horse whisperer, a guy who could talk to horses and heal them. Stu was a kind of "car whisperer"; he could tell you what was wrong with a car before popping its hood.

※

The driving snow cocooned my car. When I could no longer see through my windshield, I climbed out and looked around, sizing up my predicament. Every building on the street was dark except for one about a half block up. I trudged over the unplowed sidewalk toward the light.

A sign outside the building read THE JAVA HUT, or JAVA THE HUT, COFFEE HOUSE; because of the placement of the words on the sign, I wasn't sure which. As I approached the shop, a young woman turned the OPEN sign in the front window to CLOSED. She then walked to the front door, reaching it about the same time I did. She jumped a little when she saw me. I'm sure I was a sight, my head and shoulders frosted with snow. She was shorter than me by at least six inches, about my age, with reddish-brown hair, a wide face and fawnlike eyes the color of Coca-Cola. She was the kind of beautiful that usually tied my tongue in square knots. She opened the door just enough to stick her head out. "I'm sorry, we just closed."

I awkwardly stared at her, my hands deep in my pockets. "My car broke . . . I just need to borrow a phone."

She looked me over, then slowly stepped back and opened the door. "Come in."

I stomped the snow from my feet, then stepped inside. She locked the door behind me, as I unbuttoned my coat. "The phone's back here."

I followed her to a back office. The room was an unabashed mess. The desk was piled with paper; it looked like someone had emptied a trash pail on it. The place smelled like coffee grounds. She pointed to the phone.

"It's right there. You can sit at the desk if you want."

"Thank you. Do you have a phone book?"

"Yellow or white pages?"

"White."

She retrieved the phone book from a pile on the nearby credenza and handed it to me. I looked up the number of a friend whose brother fixed cars. I let the phone ring a dozen times then set it down. She looked at me sympathetically. "No one there?"

"I guess not."

"Do you want to call someone else?"

I couldn't think of anyone. "I don't know who I'd call."

"I know a mechanic," she said, then frowned. "But he wouldn't be there at this hour. Do you want to call a cab?"

I hadn't the money to pay for one. "No. I'll just walk."

"In this blizzard?"

"It's not far," I lied.

Her brow furrowed. "Alright. I'll let you out."

I stepped out of the office, buttoning my coat as I walked. She followed me back out to the front of the store, took out her keys and unlocked the door for me.

"Thanks anyway," I said.

"Don't mention it."

She looked at me for a moment then suddenly asked, "Are you okay?"

No one, outside of my mother, had asked me that since I left home. I'm not one to

cry—my father saw to that. Still, to my em-
barrassment, my eyes began to fill. As
much as I wanted to, I couldn't look away
from her.

"You're not, are you?" She looked at the
tears welling up in my eyes, then stepped
forward and put her arms around me. I
couldn't tell you the last time I'd had physi-
cal contact with anybody. She felt warm
and nurturing and safe. I dropped my head
on her shoulder and I openly began to cry. It
was more than a minute before I regained
my composure. I stepped back, wiping my
cheeks and feeling embarrassed to be crying in front of a complete stranger.

"I'm sorry."

"Tell me what's wrong."

I just shook my head.

She pulled a chair from a nearby table.
"Here, sit down. I'll get you a hot chocolate."

I sat down in the chair, furtively wiping my
eyes as if someone else were in the room
and might notice I'd been crying like a baby.
In a moment she came back with a steaming cup of cocoa with a cloud of whipped
cream rising above its rim.

"There you go."

I took a sip. It was hot and rich. "Thank you."

"I have a secret ingredient. I add a little maple flavoring to it."

"It's good." I looked up into her eyes. They were fixed on mine.

"What's your name?" she asked.

"Mark."

"I'm Macy."

"Macy." I repeated. "Like the parade?"

She nodded. "My father used to tell me the parade was for me."

"What's your last name?" I asked.

"Wood." She knocked on the table even though it looked to be Formica and steel. "What's yours?"

"Smart."

"That's a good name to have. From your accent I'd bet you're not from Salt Lake."

"Alabama. I came out for the U."

"Then you're a college boy," she said, sounding impressed.

"I was. Now I'm just working."

"Where do you work?"

"At West High School. I'm a custodian."

"I went to West," she said. "For a while at least." She looked at me. "Tell me what's wrong?"

"What's not?" I said. Then I breathed out deeply. "My mother died last week."

Her face fell. "I'm sorry." After a moment she reached across the table and laid her hand on mine. "Tell me about her."

"She was my best friend. No matter how bad things were, she was always there for me." I choked up again. "I didn't even go to her funeral. No one knew how to reach me, so I didn't find out about it until two days after she was buried."

"I'm so sorry," she said. After a minute she asked, "Is your family down South?"

I nodded. "Yeah."

"So you're going through all this alone."

"Yeah." I took another sip of chocolate.

"Nothing heals the soul like chocolate," she said. "I just *love* chocolate. It's God's apology for broccoli."

I smiled in spite of myself.

"There's your smile," she said softly. She sat back in her chair, watching me closely. "So you have no family here. What about friends?"

"I don't know many people in Salt Lake. I had my roommates, but when I left school . . ." I looked at her. "I had a girl-friend . . ."

"Had?"

"We were together for four years. Three days ago she wrote to tell me she's engaged."

Macy shook her head. "You weren't kidding. When it rains, it pours."

"Buckets," I said. I drank more of the hot chocolate, then turned back to her, raking my hair back with my hand. "I can't believe I'm telling you all this."

"We always tell our deepest secrets to strangers."

"Why do you think that is?"

"Maybe it's because they can't use them against us."

That made sense to me. "I feel like everything in my life has changed, like I was playing a game and someone switched boards in the middle of it. I feel like an orphan . . ."

Something about my statement seemed to affect her. "I know how that feels," she said softly.

We were quiet again and I finished my chocolate. I held up my cup: "Thank you."

"You're welcome. Do you want more?"

"No. I'm fine." I glanced down at my watch. It was now almost one. "I should let you go."

She looked at me sympathetically. "I'm still worried about you."

"I'll be fine."

"Are you sure?"

"Yes."

"Will you let me drive you home?"

I smiled at her. "If you insist."

"I do." She stood. "I just need to clean up after us." She took my cup and went back to the counter. While I sat there, she asked, "Do you want a scone? We have cranberry or cinnamon."

"No, thank you."

"How about one of our death-by-chocolate brownies? We're famous for them."

"I'm okay."

"Your loss." She came out wiping her hands on a dish towel. "I'm ready. My car's out back."

I followed her to the back door. I stepped outside while she switched off the lights, then set the alarm and shut the door. It was still snowing, but not as hard as before.

"Do you own this place?" I asked.

"No. I wish. The place is a gold mine." She locked the door and put the key in her pocket. "I'm the assistant night manager."

She pointed to a car that looked more like an igloo than a vehicle. "That's me over there. That big mound of snow," she said dolefully. "I don't have a scraper."

I looked around and found a cardboard box sticking out of the dumpster. "There's something." I tore a flap off the box, then used it to scrape the snow from the car's windows. She waited until I finished, then she unlocked the doors and we both climbed in. The car was a Ford Pinto with brown vinyl upholstery and plastic prayer beads hanging from the rearview mirror. The plastic dashboard was cracked in places and bandaged with assorted decals, mostly from radio stations. It took several turns of the key before the engine turned over. The windshield was fogged, and Macy revved the engine a couple times then turned on the defroster. The air gradually turned warm. My hands were wet and red from scraping snow, and she reached over and lightly rubbed them.

"Your hands are freezing. Thanks for cleaning the snow off."

"You're welcome."

"Don't mind my car. It's held together with prayer and duct tape."

"At least it runs."

"That's right, be grateful it runs." She shoved a cassette into her stereo and soft music began playing. "Where do you live?"

"I'm over on Third South. Just over the viaduct."

"I thought you said it was close."

"I didn't want to trouble you."

While we waited for the windshield to clear, she reached into the back seat and brought up an open box of ginger snaps. "Want a snap?"

"Sure." I reached in the box and took one. She took one as well.

"I love these things," she said.

When the windshield was defrosted enough to see through, she put the car in gear and we slowly pulled out from the parking lot onto the road, fishtailing a little.

"This is scary," she said. "I can't believe we got this much snow." She reached down and turned up the heater. After fifteen minutes of precarious driving I pointed to the large rundown house where I lived.

"It's right there. That house up ahead."

Macy sided the car up to the curb under a streetlamp. She left the engine running but pulled the parking brake. "You sure you're okay?"

"I'll be fine. Thank you. For everything."

"It's nothing." She suddenly smiled. "I have something for you." She reached across me to the glove box, brought out a card and handed it to me. "That's for a free pastry and coffee at the café. You have to try one of our famous brownies sometime."

I slid the card into my shirt pocket. "Thanks." I looked at her. "Why are you being so good to me?"

She smiled and I saw something both beautiful and sad in her eyes. "You seem like a really nice guy who just had a lot of bad things happen to him all at once."

I looked down for a moment and slowly exhaled. Then I looked back into her eyes. "You might have saved my life tonight."

"I know." She reached over and again touched my hand. "All bad things pass with time. You can trust me on that."

I cupped her hand with mine. "Thank you."

"My pleasure. Take care of yourself," she said.

"You too. Good night." I stepped out of her car onto the curb and shut the door behind me. She pulled into the road, made a U-turn and waved once more before she drove off, disappearing behind a curtain of snow. My mother was right. Angels do walk the earth.

CHAPTER
Three

I went back looking for Macy.
Apparently she doesn't exist.

✦ MARK SMART'S DIARY ✦

I couldn't get Macy out of my mind. I even dreamed about her. I felt as if I'd been sleepwalking through the past few days, and part of me wondered if I had really seen her or if she'd been the light at the end of a nightmare. Either way I knew I had to see her again.

I borrowed my landlord's phone and got through to the mechanic on my first call. He agreed to meet me at my car around noon, a little more than an hour from then. I quickly showered and dressed, then ran to catch the bus.

The blizzard had passed, leaving the valley still and buried in snow. The sun was out but apparently just for show, as the air bit fiercely, turning my cheeks and ears red as I waited at the bus stop. The bus dropped me off just a few blocks east of the coffee shop, and I walked past it toward my car. The city snowplows had been by in the night and snow had been pushed clear up to my car's windows. I now realized that I had stopped in a no-parking zone, but I couldn't tell if I had a parking ticket. At least it hadn't been towed. In truth, my thoughts were less on my car than they were on Macy. I checked my watch. I still had ten minutes to noon. The mechanic hadn't arrived, so I walked into the café.

The place was crowded, and as I looked around I suddenly felt a little anxious. What would I say to her? What if she didn't want to see me again? I mean, you might give a panhandler a dollar, but you don't necessarily want to bring him home for dinner.

I went to the back of the line at the cash register. When I reached the front, a young woman with eyes rimmed with dark mascara and wearing a Bruce Springsteen T-shirt looked up and smiled at me. "What can I get for you, honey?"

"I'm looking for Macy."

She looked at me blankly. "Macy?"

"Yes."

"Am I supposed to know who that is?"

"She works here."

Her brow creased. "I don't know any Macy. Do you mean Mary?"

"No, Macy. She works the night shift."

The woman shook her head. "Mary works the night shift." She turned to a coworker who was pounding coffee grounds from a grate. "You know of any Macy who works here?"

"Macy?"

"Yeah."

"You mean Mary?"

She turned to me. "You sure you don't mean Mary?"

"No, it's Macy. Like the department store."

"What does she look like?"

"She's small. Has short auburn hair. Big eyes. Really pretty."

"That's Mary."

"What's her last name?" I asked.

"Hummel."

"No, her last name is Wood."

"There's no one named Wood here."

I didn't know what to say. The woman looked at me with pity, and I guessed she was thinking I had asked for the name of one of her coworkers and had been given a fake one. Or maybe I just thought that.

"Sorry I can't help you. Do you want anything else?"

I felt stupid. "I guess I'll have a hot chocolate," I said.

"That I can help you with. With whipped
cream or without?"

"With."

"What size?"

"Small."

I paid for the chocolate and picked it up a
minute later. I sat down near the front window where I could watch for the mechanic.
About the time I finished my drink, a beat-
up Chevy truck pulled up in front of my car.
As I walked out, a man hopped from the
cab. He wore work boots, mustard-colored
overalls, no coat but a knit cap and a white
turtleneck.

I walked out to greet him. "Hi. I'm Mark."
My breath froze in front of me.

"Carl," he said.

"Thanks for coming."

"Yeah." He looked at my snow-piled
car. "I've got a couple brooms in back." He
took two push brooms from his truck bed,
handed me one, and we brushed the snow
from my windows, door and hood. Then he
knelt down and hooked a nylon tow rope to
the front of my bumper and the tow ball of

his pickup. With some difficulty, I pulled open the driver's side door.

"You been pulled before?" he asked.

"Yes." Actually, on more occasions than I could account for. Stu was always helping folks who couldn't afford tow trucks. I have to give him credit for that; even though we didn't have much money, he was always helping people out. He once refused payment from a single mother who lived down the road from us, telling her that the problem with her car was nothing but a dirty spark plug. He had actually spent the better part of the morning rebuilding her carburetor. Being only ten, I was about to say something, but a stern glance from him shut me up.

✳

"Just keep the rope tight," Carl shouted from the cab's open window. "Don't forget to put your car in neutral. And release the parking brake if you got it on."

"Got it," I said, climbing inside. My car was as cold as a meat locker. I found that the battery had died and I had no wipers or heater. When the road was clear, he stuck his arm out to signal, then his truck lurched forward, yanking my car from the bank sideways out into the street. Twenty minutes later we arrived at his home. He pulled me into his driveway. I set the brake and climbed out.

I gave him my keys, then used his phone to call Victor, a guy who cleaned the school with me. Victor had offered to pick me up if I ever needed a ride. It was an offer that up until now I had declined for two reasons: First, I had my own car and didn't need a ride. Second, all conversations with Victor inevitably devolved into discussions about UFOs and conspiracy theories. You could be talking about the weather, and he'd bring it around to a diatribe on the government's cover-up of a flying saucer found in Los Alamos, New Mexico. I rarely agreed (actually never) with his beliefs, and I suspect he believed I was either a dupe or willfully collaborating with some secret government agency that monitors the actions of extraterrestrials here on earth.

*

Victor arrived about forty-five minutes later and, spurred on by a captive audience, was in good form on our drive into work, covering all the basics of UFO lore, from alien abductions and crop circles to unexplained cow mutilations in southern Utah. He had added something to his repertoire: spontaneous human combustion— informing me that at least twenty-six people spontaneously burst into flames each year and he had taken to carrying a fire extinguisher in the back of his car. He gave me permission to use it on him should he suddenly burst into flames. I suggested we have a practice run, but he found no humor in this.

Victor didn't stop talking even after we arrived at the school. Still, the time passed quickly, with my mind pleasantly engaged somewhere else. I suppose the heart, like nature, abhors a vacuum, and I had found something, or someone, to put into it. Based on my curious noontime experience at the café, I knew it was possible that I might not ever see Macy again, but still it was pleasant thinking about her.

It was nearly 11 P.M. when Victor dropped me back off at the mechanic's house. My car was parked out front, which

I decided was a good sign. The home was dark except for the glow from the front room television. I knocked on the door. A minute later Carl opened, his hair matted and his eyes glazed from too much TV.

"Sorry it's so late," I said. "I just got off work."

He rubbed his neck. "It's okay. I got her running."

"Great." I waved to Victor and he drove off. "So what was wrong?"

"Timing belt busted. And your battery was dead."

I remembered enough from the auto shop to know this was expensive news. "How much do I owe you?"

"You got lucky; I found a belt at the junk-yard. Fifty bucks for parts and seventy for my time. I didn't charge you for charging your battery."

"Thanks," I said, reaching for my wallet. "I've got cash." I paid him six twenties. It should have been double that. Still it was almost all I had. I'd be eating peanut butter sandwiches and breakfast cereal for the next week.

"Your keys are under the seat. Door's not locked."

"Thanks. Have a good night."

"Yeah." He shut the door.

I started my car and drove home.

CHAPTER
Four

Jam yesterday and Jam tomorrow.
What can I do to hide my sorrow?
Wonderland is gone,
somehow Alice went wrong . . .

✦ SONG LYRICS FROM MARK SMART'S DIARY ✦

The place I lived was an old two-story Tudor that had been converted into rental units. I lived in the smallest apartment: a studio with a shower-bath with a plastic curtain (illustrated with toaster-sized cartoon goldfish) and a kitchen with a tile sink and counter and a small hot plate. There was no oven, but I didn't care since I wasn't really keen on cooking anyway. Rent was only $175 a month, which was good since I didn't earn much. Even though it was almost midnight, I sat down with my guitar, running my fingers up the smooth back of its varnished neck. I gently strummed it, tuned the third string, then began playing a song I had started writing right after learning my mother had died. I softly sang,

*Alice never went back through the
   looking glass,
And Wonderland never was the same.*

*I think back on memories of my
    childhood years,
But I never can go back again.*

*If I could take all the hopes of
    childhood,
The wishes and dreams I once knew,
I'd gather them all if I had the chance,
And trade them back for you.*

*And Wonderland is gone,
Somehow Alice went wrong,
I think I could find her if I really tried,
But maybe I just don't belong . . .*

I finished strumming mid-chord, letting the guitar's echo die in the room. I don't know why I was torturing myself. Thinking about my mother was hard enough, let alone singing about her. *Therapy,* I told myself.

Just then there was a knock on my door. I grimaced. *Landlord,* I thought. My landlord was a peculiar duck. He was in his late seventies, and he lived alone in the apartment directly above me. When I was still deciding on the apartment, he had generously offered me the use of his telephone, an offer he conveniently forgot the first time I asked to use it.

Also, he went to bed early, usually around eight, and was a light sleeper. He hated that I worked late; claiming I always woke him, no matter how quiet I tried to be. If he heard anything from me past ten o'clock, he was down, red-faced and ranting. I laid my guitar next to the couch, then unlocked the dead bolt, bracing for his tirade. I pulled open the door. Macy stood in the dark hallway. For a moment we just stared at each other.

"Did I wake you?" she asked.

"No, I just got home. Come in."

"Thanks." She stepped inside, casually surveying the room. Her gaze stopped on my guitar. "Was that you singing?"

"It's just a song I've been working on."

"You wrote that?" she asked, sounding impressed.

"Yes."

"You're very good."

Her praise pleased me. I walked over to my couch and moved my guitar case. "Have a seat."

She came over and sat back into my couch. "Nice place. Cozy." She reached over and touched my guitar. "Do you teach guitar?"

"I used to, back in Alabama. I've thought of getting started here, but my life has been so disjointed lately . . . it's hard to find students."

"I've always wanted to take lessons," she said. She looked back at me. "Sorry to come by so late. I just got off work and I wanted to see how you were doing."

"I'm doing okay."

"Really?"

"Really. Thanks to you. I've felt like a madman this past week. You breathed sanity back into me."

She smiled. "Good."

"I'm surprised you found my place. It was midnight in the middle of a blizzard when you dropped me off."

"I got a little lost. But just for a moment."

"Were you at the . . . coffee shop?"

"Yes."

"You know, I'm not really sure what your coffee shop is called."

"That's okay, no one does."

"What do you mean?"

"When it first opened, it was called the Java Hut. Then, like five years ago, Jeff, the owner's son, took over. He's all into science fiction and *Star Wars* and he thought it would be cool to change the name around to Java the Hut; you know, like Jabba the Hut, that big lizard guy in the *Star Wars* movie. I don't think people even make the connection anymore, but most people just call it the Hut anyway."

"Jeff would like Victor," I said.

"Who?"

"No one," I said quickly. "I came by . . . *the Hut* . . . when I got my car this morning. I wanted to see if you were there."

"I only work the night shift."

"When I asked about you, they said there wasn't a Macy Wood working there."

"That's because everyone thinks my name is Mary Hummel."

"Why would they think that?"

"It's what's on my Social Security card and that's what my boss put on the work schedule when I first started . . . It doesn't matter, I answer to about anything."

"How do you go from Macy Wood to Mary Hummel?"

"I have kind of a"—she hesitated—"interesting life."

"Interesting as in fascinating or interesting as in a nightmare?"

"Yes."

I nodded slowly. "Last night, when I told you I felt like an orphan, you said you knew what I meant. Did you also lose your parents?" She looked away from me, seemingly uncomfortable with my question. "If you don't want to talk about it . . ."

"No, it's all right." She looked back up and smiled sadly. "Actually it's more like they lost me."

"What do you mean?"

"When I was seven, I was given up for adoption."

I wasn't sure how to respond. Finally I said, "I'm sorry."

"It was pretty tough, but I was a pretty tough kid by then. My parents were alcoholics and drug addicts. I had been in and out of foster homes and drug rehabilitation centers so many times the only constant in my life was change. When I was seven, the state intervened and I was adopted by the Hummels. Mrs. Hummel didn't like the name Macy, so she changed the *c* to an *r*. Mrs. Hummel wasn't a very nice lady. I ran away from home at fifteen and haven't been back since. Mary Hummel is my legal name, but my real name is Macy Wood."

"Where did you live after you ran away?"

"Mostly at friends' homes. I just kind of sofa-hopped for a year or so. Then when my friends started leaving home themselves, I spent a few months on the street. Those were the worst days. But like they say, it's always darkest before dawn. That's when I met Jo."

Revealingly, my heart sank. "Joe's your boyfriend?"

She smiled. "No. Jo's a woman. Actually her real name is Joette."

"Joette?"

"It's what happens when your parents are named Joe and Yvette and they only have one child. I was busing tables at a Denny's and she was a waitress there. She said she was looking for a roommate to help with expenses. She only charged me twenty-five dollars a month. It wasn't until I was older that I figured out she was really just trying to get me off the street. I eventually quit Denny's and came to the Hut, but I still live with Jo. She's looked after me ever since."

"I never would have guessed your life had been that hard."

"Why?"

"Because you're so . . ."

"Normal?" she offered.

"I was going to say *nice*."

"Just too many scars to jest at wounds." She sighed. "Well, that was a lot more of my history than I planned to share. So I guess we're even."

"It happens." After a moment I asked, "Is there anyone else in your family?"

"A little sister," she said softly.

"How has she fared?"

"I don't know. I haven't seen her since I was adopted."

After a minute I asked. "Have you ever thought of trying to find her?"

"A few times. Especially recently. I've been having these dreams. I'm at a public swimming pool and I hear a little girl calling for me like she's drowning. I go to help her when Mrs. Hummel grabs me and carries me away." She looked at me. "I don't know why I've been having them."

"Maybe it's a sign."

"I've wondered that.The thing is I don't really know where I'd start. Or maybe I'm just afraid of what I might find. Or not find."

She sighed again then looked down at her watch. "I better go."

We got up together and she stopped at my doorway. "I'm glad you're doing better."

"Thanks for checking up on me. Could I have your phone number?"

"Sure."

I grabbed the first piece of paper I could find—I think it was a tract from the Watchtower Society—and she wrote her number down on the back of it.

"I'll walk you out," I said.

Outside, Macy lingered at her car, searching through her purse for her keys. When she found them, she looked back up, leaned forward and hugged me. When we parted, she looked into my face.

"I'd like to hear you play your guitar sometime."

"Are you busy tomorrow night?"

She frowned. "I'm working."

"How about Friday?"

"I have to work every night this week. Actually, all I do is work." Then her face lit. "I have an idea. Every Thursday night we have live entertainment. It's usually Carlos, this old hippie guy who plays the guitar. But the last couple of weeks he's been out with bronchitis or something. You should come play. We'll hang out afterwards."

"I've never really performed in public," I said. "Outside of my sophomore talent show. But it sounds fun. I don't get off work until seven. Would seven-thirty be okay?"

"That's perfect. We have a sound system. So you just need to bring your guitar. And it pays ten dollars an hour plus tips."

"I'll see you there."

"Good night." She climbed into her car and I stood there until she had driven away. Then I walked back inside amazed at how happy this girl made me.

CHAPTER
Five

I've wondered why it is that some people come through difficult times bitter and broken while others emerge stronger and more empathetic? I've read that the same breeze that extinguishes some flames just fans others. I still don't know what kind of flame I am.

✦MARK SMART'S DIARY✦

DECEMBER 3, 1974

There was something different this time. Even at the age of seven, Macy had developed a sense about these things. In the last year she had bounced in and out of foster homes with such frequency that she had already lived with seven different families. But this time there was something about the confederacy of big people that set off warning signals inside her head as shrill as a school bell. Where was her little sister?

A squat, melon-faced woman with dyed yellow hair looked at her flatly, a cloud of smoke billowing up from the cigarette clamped between her teeth. She wore a thick black wool coat that fell to her shins and fit her body like a cover on a barbeque grill. The only color she wore was a Christmas tree broach with bright red and green faux jewels. The woman's eyes emotionlessly crawled over her while the other two adults, her father and the woman from the state, seemed to avoid looking at her at all.

✳

It was late afternoon. Macy rocked on her heels, occasionally kicking a little at the snow with her oversized red Converse sneakers.

She had sensed that something would happen today. Yesterday was a good day, maybe the best in years, and experience had proven there was always something suspicious about that. She had spent the day with her father, just the two of them, on an all-day daddy-daughter date. She had asked where her Sissy was, but her father said this was a special day for just them. They had gone to a movie and bought popcorn and Raisinets. Afterward, they had gone down to the dollar store where there were more treats: a caramel apple, a pencil with a jack-o'-lantern eraser, a candy valentine's heart, a green shamrock: every special day of the year combined into one. Then her father had carried her home on his shoulders, a rare treat, for he still limped from his childhood bout with polio. They had chattered and played all day, blissfully ignoring the question she knew would be answered in time. Life had taught her that no good day went unpaid for.

Her father wore the same clothes as the day before: the tan down vest, the motor-oil-stained T-shirt not quite concealing the tattoos on his upper arm. Still he looked different now.

The woman from the state looked like a giant to her—taller than her father by nearly a head—gaunt in the face, her cheeks pale, her nose red from the cold. She was a caseworker and Macy had seen many of them. Most of them had been kind or sympathetic, others frantic or burned out, but to Macy they were all the same—ushers to new unwelcome worlds, away from her family's problems.

Always there were *problems.* She didn't understand why caseworkers and foster parents had to be a part of *their family's problems.* Ever since her mother died, their problems had gotten worse. Much worse. Why didn't her father just stop using the drugs that made the problems and these people come? Why didn't the caseworkers take the drugs away instead of her?

.*.

The tall woman finished speaking to her father, then turned to Macy, crouching down on her haunches so that she was only slightly taller than the little girl. "Macy, this is Mrs. Irene Hummel. Mrs. Hummel is your new mother."

Macy glanced furtively at Mrs. Hummel, then to her father, and his expression did not change with the caseworker's words. *Mother?* This woman didn't look like any mother she would want.

"I had a mother, thank you," she said meekly, hoping against experience that something she said might make a difference.

Mrs. Hummel blew out a large puff of smoke, briefly obscuring her face.

"You're very lucky," the caseworker said. Most kids over four never get *adopted.*" The caseworker stood back up and it seemed that she was even taller now. "It's time to say goodbye."

Her father knelt down next to her. "You okay, sport?"

She tried to act brave but her stomach hurt. "What about Sissy?"

"She's not going with you."

"Who will take care of her?"

"She'll be okay."

Tears welled up in her eyes. "She needs me."

"She'll be okay."

"But I don't want to go."

"I know." There was futility in his eyes and Macy knew it would happen. It always happened the way the grown-ups said it would. "I have something for you. You fell asleep before I could give it to you last night." He handed her a box containing a bright red glass Christmas ornament. Written in glitter were the words NOEL. DECEMBER 25. She looked at it, then wiped her face with her mittens.

"It's from Mom," he said.

"Thank you." She took the box in her hands.

He exhaled loudly, then stood. There was a quick glance between her father and the yellow-haired woman. The woman said to Macy. "C'mon."

Macy looked at her father and the caseworker with hope, but neither would look at her. So she picked up the black plastic garbage bag filled with her clothes and followed the woman, who was already walking to her car. The car was pieced together with body panels from at least three different automobiles, all of different colors: dull metallic blue, brown and lime green. Macy opened the back door, threw her bag on the seat opposite her, then climbed into the car and fastened her seat belt. The seats were ripped in places and the foam rubber protruded, enmeshed between springs. The car reeked of cigarette smoke in spite of the tree-shaped air freshener that hung from the rearview mirror.

The woman started the car, then reached down and turned on the radio to a country station. Macy glanced back once more at her father. The caseworker was talking to him and he looked at the ground. Then, as the car started to move, he looked into her eyes once, then looked away. And then he was gone. Macy closed her eyes tightly and tried not to cry out loud.

✦

Ten minutes into the drive the woman turned down the radio.

"You had lunch?"

"Yes, ma'am," she lied. She hadn't eaten since breakfast. Eating was one area of her life where she felt control.

"You're skinny as a paper clip."

"Yes, ma'am."

"Case you're wondering, you have a sister and two brothers."

Macy just stared out the window in silence. Her mind reeled in ways she couldn't explain. She had developed mechanisms to cope with her fear, and she had retreated into herself, or perhaps out of herself, as she felt as if she were outside her body, watching this little girl thrown into a frightening new world. The woman just sucked on her cigarette. She had expended all the effort she would in conversation.

The ride seemed interminable.

Twenty-five minutes later the car passed a supermarket and turned down a narrow dead-end road. The second house from the end was a small, prefabricated home with green aluminum siding and a gray shingle roof. The front porch was elevated and it had an aluminum-awning covering. The picture window to the side of the porch had been broken and there was cardboard duct-taped to it on the inside. The yard was filled with weeds, and to the side of the house were cars in various stages of cannibalization. As they pulled in to the driveway, the woman said, "This is your new home."

"It's very nice," Macy said. She had learned to always say this because it made the big people happy. But if it affected this woman at all, she couldn't tell.

The woman shut off the car and opened the door. She threw what was left of her cigarette on the ground then climbed out. "Get your things."

"Yes, ma'am."

Macy followed her to the front porch. The aluminum outer door was missing a panel. There was a cardboard sign over the doorbell that read BROKE. It was stuck to the wooden frame with a flesh-colored Band-Aid. The door had been scribbled on with crayon.

The woman opened the door and shouted, "We're back," as she walked inside.

Macy stepped in behind her onto the vinyl parquet floor entry. The front room was small, the floor covered with tan shag carpet. There was a peculiar smell to the room, like dog, though the odor was mostly obscured by the clinging stench of cigarettes. There was a Christmas tree in the corner of the room, decorated with a red felt tree skirt, colorful ornaments and strands of popcorn, and in spite of everything else this made Macy happy. Maybe they would let her hang her new ornament on the tree as well.

✦

A girl and two boys ran into the room. The girl was stout, slightly younger than Macy and bore a resemblance to the woman. Standing behind the girl one boy appeared to be Macy's age, the other a few years older. They all stared at her as if she were some new species of animal. For a moment no one spoke. Then the girl said, "That's not Buffy."

The woman took off her coat, hooking it to a coat tree. "I told you *Buffy* was already taken."

Macy glanced back and forth between them. *Who was Buffy?*

"I wanted *Buffy.*"

"You'll take *her.*"

"What's her name?" the older boy asked.

"I'm Macy," she said trying to sound cheerful.

"Stupid name," the younger boy said.

"Not as stupid as *Buffy,*" the older boy said, laughing. "Boooooffeeee," he said, taunting his sister.

"You said I could have Buffy for Christmas," the girl whined.

"Just shut up," the woman said. "Buffy's gone. Someone else got her."

"What are your names?" Macy asked.

"Bart," said the oldest. "He's Ronny and that's Sheryl."

"Hi, guys," Macy said brightly.

No one answered. Just then a dog came into the room. It was large—gigantic to Macy—with brown, brindled fur. Its head looked awkwardly large for its body. It stopped when it saw Macy and a deep, fierce growl rose from its throat.

Macy took a step back. She was afraid of dogs. Especially this one.

"Buster don't like new people," Bart said.

"Eat her, Buster," Ronny said.

Macy froze with fear. The dog's ears fell back and it barked loud enough to hurt Macy's ears.

"Get that dog outta here," the woman shouted at Bart.

"She's a pit bull," Bart said to Macy. "They call them that cuz they made them for fightin' in pits. She could kill you in one second flat."

"I said get! And clean up his mess on the back porch."

"It's not my turn."

"I don't care whose turn it is, I told you to do it."

"Make the new girl do it," Ronny said.

"Yeah," Bart said to Macy. "That's your new job, cleaning up after Buster."

"Now!" the woman screamed.

Bart groaned, then grabbed the dog by the collar and began dragging it away. "C'mon, Buster."

The woman turned to Sheryl. "Now show her the room."

Sheryl defiantly crossed her arms. "She can't sleep in my room."

The woman shot a fierce glance at the girl and she wilted beneath it.

"Okay, *fine,*" Sheryl said.

Mrs. Hummel walked from the room. Sheryl turned to Macy, her face screwed up in anger and defeat. "C'mon."

Macy looked back at the front door. She could run away from these ugly, mean people, but to where? She had no idea where she was. She lifted her plastic bag.

"Why you carrying a garbage sack?" Ronny asked.

"Nun' your business," Macy said.

He looked at her ornament. "What's in your hand?"

"Nun' your business."

He moved toward her. "Give it to me."

Macy looked him in the eyes. She let the sack fall to the ground, then balled her fist. "Touch it and I'll knock you clear into tomorrow."

Ronny paused, uncertain of whether or not she could but pretty certain she'd try. Macy had fought bigger boys. Boys at the drug rehabilitation centers who wanted to do things to her or her sister. She had won some of those fights, or at least made enough trouble to deter them. But there were times that she lost and they did what they wanted. She had never felt so vulnerable as when she was being *protected* by the state.

Ronny, ashamed at being backed down, walked out of the room. Macy followed

Sheryl to the bedroom. It was a box of a room, cramp and cluttered, the floor littered with clothes and foam rubber chunks from a cushion the dog had gotten at. There was a bunk bed in the corner of the room.

"You sleep on top. Unless you wet the bed. You wet the bed?"

"No."

"Better not."

Sheryl left the room. Macy threw her bag on the top bunk, then looked around for a place to hide her ornament. Another world, another uncertainty. One thing she knew for certain—she would leave the first chance she got.

CHAPTER
Six

Macy has decided to find her sister which might be a little tricky seeing how she can't even remember her sister's name. I have a feeling that somehow her journey will involve me. I can't imagine a better travel companion.

✦ MARK SMART'S DIARY ✦

I showed up at the Hut a few minutes before seven. I parked next to Macy's car in the back lot and entered by the employee's entrance, a black metal door decorated with bumper stickers. I had my guitar slung across my back, its bright yellow strap crossing my chest. Macy had been waiting for me and smiled when she saw me. She took my hand, leading me to the same office where I had made the phone call. This time a man, mid-forties and balding, occupied the desk.

"Jeff, this is Mark."

Jeff glanced up at me. "Pleasure," he said with impersonal cordiality. "You got a big crowd tonight."

"Thanks for letting me play."

"You betcha," he said. "You know any Christmas songs?"

"Not for the guitar."

"Maybe you could learn some." He returned to his calculator.

Macy led me out.

"Christmas songs?" I said.

"He's trying to push holiday gift sales. Just be glad he didn't ask if you could play the *Star Wars* theme."

"I'm glad for all of us."

In the corner of the room was a black vinyl-upholstered stool set behind a chrome microphone stand. The mike was plugged in to a small suitcase-size amp. A light on the amp glowed amber.

"I have something for you." She lifted a flyer from a nearby table. It read:

Guitar Lessons from Mark Smart
Reasonably Priced
Call 445-3989

"I assumed you were reasonably priced. If you're not, you can just write 'un' in front of 'reasonably'. I put my own number down until you get a phone."

Again I was amazed at her thoughtfulness. "Thanks."

"Let me know if you need anything else. Knock us dead."

As she went back behind the counter, I unlatched my case and lifted out my guitar, leaving the case open for tips. When I thought no one was looking, I dropped in a five-dollar bill of my own. Priming the pump.

I straddled the vinyl stool. Nearly every seat in the place was taken and everyone seemed content in their own conversations, unaware of my presence. I felt like I was intruding. Maybe they'd tip me *not* to play.

I adjusted the chrome microphone stand, then tapped the microphone. It was dead. I found the switch and turned it on. There was instant feedback, a shrill screech that brought the place to a standstill, like the amplified sound of nails scraping across a chalkboard. I lunged at the mike and shut it off, nearly dropping my guitar in the process. If I had wanted to be unobtrusive, I had just blown it. I glanced over at the counter and Macy was grinning.

I moved the microphone a safe distance from the amp, danced my fingers through a few silent chords, then started lightly picking until it felt good, and I started into a song. At first some of the customers glanced over at me but just as quickly returned to their lattes and conversations. My first song, a James Taylor number, received polite applause. *At least no one threw any-*

thing. I played a couple more songs, and with each one I brought a few more of the customers in. About a half hour later I felt confident enough to speak to the crowd.

"I'd like to play something I wrote. This is a song for my mother."

Several of those at the closest tables turned their chairs toward me. I played the song Macy had heard me practicing when she came to my apartment. This time when I finished, everyone in the room clapped. I looked over and even the workers were watching. Macy gave me a thumbs up. A couple of women, one blond, the other a redhead, got up to leave but first walked out of their way toward me. The blonde dropped three dollar bills into my case. "That was great," she said.

"Yeah," said the other. "Will you be here next Thursday?"

"I'm not sure. I'm just filling in for someone."

"We know," said the blonde. "We're regulars. We hope you come back."

"I've been thinking of taking guitar lessons," said the redhead. "Are you taking new students?"

"Of course he is," said the blonde. "Why else would he have a flyer?"

"If you give me your number," I said, "I'll call and we can arrange a lesson."

She wrote her number down on a napkin and handed it to me.

"She was hoping you'd ask for her number," the blonde said.

"You're going to be walking home," the redhead told her friend. She turned back to me, "Thanks."

"No problem."

They left the café.

By the end of the night the bottom of my guitar case was littered with bills and silver coins. I had exhausted my repertoire and was playing the same songs from earlier in the night, but the place had mostly cleared out except for Macy and a woman behind the counter. At midnight Macy locked the doors. I put away my guitar and counted my tips, stuffing the wad into my coat pocket. When Macy had finished cleaning, she came and sat next to me, bringing me a cup of hot chocolate with whipped cream. "Everyone liked you," she said. "Even Jeff was impressed. He said you can come back."

"I'd love to."

"How'd you make out on tips?"

"Almost fifty dollars."

"That's *really* good. I think Carlos usually does twenty-something."

"I don't think people like Carlos."

"No. He's about twenty years past his prime. You're a good replacement."

"And two people asked about lessons."

"I'm not surprised. It's my flyer. It was . . . compelling."

"It was compelling." I laughed. "Can I take you to dinner?"

"How about breakfast? I'm craving pancakes."

"Pancakes it is."

We drove to a nearby IHOP. I ordered fries and Macy ordered a large stack of buttermilk pancakes, which she drowned in a sea of maple syrup. It was amusing to see someone that small with such a large appetite.

"I've been thinking a lot about what you said the other night," Macy said. "I'm going to do it."

"Do what?"

"Find my sister."

"Cool. So where do you start?"

"I called the DCFS this morning. I have an appointment with a caseworker tomorrow at ten."

"What's DCFS?"

"Division of Child and Family Services. They're the ones who took me from home." She looked down and cut a piece of pancake. "Do you know what I really hate? I hate that I can't even remember her name." She shook her head emphatically. "I can't remember my own sister's *name*." She lifted the fork to her mouth.

"Maybe there's a reason," I said.

"Like because I was only seven?"

"Or maybe being separated was so traumatic, you blocked it out. I did a paper on this in high school. It's called repression. The more traumatic the experience, the more likely it is to happen."

She finished chewing. "You should be a psychiatrist."

"I have too many issues."

"All psychiatrists have issues. Why do you think they became psychiatrists?"

We finished eating, I paid the check and we went out to our cars. We had driven separately so we said goodbye in the parking lot.

"Thanks for breakfast."

"Thanks for everything you did for me tonight. That was a lot of fun. I don't know how to repay you."

"I should make you give me a cut of your tips," she said, smiling. "But I'll settle for a discount on guitar lessons."

"For you it's free."

"No, you have to charge me *something*."

"No, I don't."

"I insist."

"Then you can pay me in hot chocolate."

"How about once a week I make you dinner and then we have a lesson?"

"That's fair."

"Well, don't be too sure. You haven't tasted my cooking."

"It's got to be better than mine."

She smiled. "It's a deal then."

"I'll call you tomorrow."

"I'll be waiting. Good night."

We hugged. As we parted, I said, "Tell me something."

"Yes?"

"Why did you come back to check up on me?"

She thought about it. "I don't know. I just liked you. And you're pretty cute." She smiled and climbed into her car. "Talk to you tomorrow."

I waited until she'd driven off before starting my car. I'd known her for just four days and I was already falling in love.

CHAPTER
Seven

When it comes to hurting children we cannot claim ignorance. Every adult I've ever met has once been a child. And some have become more so.

✦ MARK SMART'S DIARY ✦

NOVEMBER 30, 1975

Macy sat in the back seat of the car, pushed up against the door. She was dressed in a red and green plaid Christmas dress with puffy sleeves and a skirt that flared out like a bell. It was the first time she'd worn a dress since she had come to the Hummel home. It was also the first time Mrs. Hummel had taken an interest in how Macy looked. She had scrubbed her cheeks so hard they were still red.

The four children in the back seat of the Dodge Charger were all dressed up in what Irene Hummel called their "Sunday meeting clothes," which was peculiar since they never went anywhere on Sunday, church meetings or otherwise. To Macy it felt like they were playacting and these were the costumes.

Macy's adoptive father, Dick, was driving. Dick Hummel was a baker at a midsized supermarket. He was a quiet man, low-key and unemotional, and the one person Macy got along with at home. Macy sensed that he felt sorry for her—or perhaps for both of them. In spite of their age difference, between them developed a peculiar camaraderie not dissimilar to that among victims of any disaster.

Unfortunately he was rarely home. Macy didn't blame him for being gone so much. She wouldn't be there either if she had a choice. She once asked Dick if she could go to work with him, but Mrs. Hummel vetoed it. "It's just her little scheme to get out of her chores," she said. Mrs. Hummel always acted funny when Macy spent time with Dick.

Macy's thoughts were suddenly broken by an elbow to her ribs. "If the judge asks me, I'm going to tell him we don't want you," Bart said.

"Me too," said Sheryl.

Macy turned back to the window. "Fine with me," she said.

*

When they walked into the courthouse, the social worker who had taken her from her father was there to greet her. Macy hadn't seen her in almost a year, not since she had sent her to the Hummels'. Now she acted as familiar as family. *More playacting.*

"You look so nice," she said to Macy, a smile plastered across her face. "What a special day. You are so *lucky.*"

There must be another meaning to the word that I don't know, Macy thought. Then she had a hopeful thought. Perhaps the judge would ask her if she wanted to be adopted. She would tell him that everyone was mean to her. That Mrs. Hummel yelled at her all the time and sometimes slapped her and made her do more work than the other kids. Maybe then they'd let her go back to her father.

"We have a surprise for you," the caseworker announced with a broad smile. "Your sister is going to be adopted with you."

Macy's heart leapt. Finally something good had happened in her life. "You mean we get to live together?"

The woman's smile disappeared. "No. I meant she's just being adopted at the same time. We thought you would like that."

Ten minutes later Macy's little sister

came into the room. She was immaculately dressed in a navy velvet dress, her hair perfectly groomed and pulled back with a silk ribbon. She was flanked by two well-mannered little boys dressed in matching navy suits and clip-on neckties. They looked like small replicas of their father, a handsome, well-dressed man in a navy pinstriped suit with a crisp white shirt and silk necktie.

Noel screamed when she saw her sister. "Macy," she cried. "Macy, Macy!" They ran to each other, colliding in the center of the room. The Hummels and Noel's parents, the Thorups, kept their distance, sitting on opposite ends of the vestibule. Noel had had trouble dealing with Macy's absence and a child psychologist suggested to the Thorups that they allow the two girls to spend some time together. Mrs. Thorup contacted Mrs. Hummel to discuss the situation, and what started as a simple request escalated into a shouting match between the two women. Mrs. Hummel would not allow Macy to see her sister. The dislike the two families felt toward each other was palpable.

✶

"Don't go 'way," Noel said. Macy held her tightly, both of them oblivious to the adults who watched from both sides of the room.

"I won't, Sissy."

The two little girls sat together on the tile floor, and for that time, all was well with the world; Macy made faces and Noel laughed.

Twenty minutes later the caseworker came into the room. She said to Mr. and Mrs. Hummel, "The judge is ready to see you."

Mrs. Hummel impatiently bounded from her chair and walked to Macy, putting her hands on her shoulders. "C'mon," she said.

Macy looked at her sister and began to cry. "I don't want to go."

"No, no, no!" Noel screamed at Mrs. Hummel. "She's my Macy. You can't have her!"

Mr. Thorup walked up to take her. "Come on, honey. Macy needs to go now."

Noel erupted in a piercing scream. "No! Don't go!" She grabbed tightly onto Macy's waist. "Don't go! Don't go!"

Irene Hummel looked at the man as if the

situation was his fault. "We need to go," she said. "Control your daughter."

The man glared back at her. "Give her a break, lady. They're sisters." He gently lifted Noel by the waist. "Come on, hon."

"Macy! Macy! Don't go!"

Macy began crying. "I don't want to go."

As Mr. Thorup pulled, Noel clutched all the more desperately to the skirt of Macy's dress. He stood awkwardly in the center of the room, holding the little girl horizontally as she screamed loud enough to be heard anywhere on the floor, and city employees looked out of their offices to see the commotion.

"Muzzle that brat," Irene shouted.

"Someone should muzzle you," the man said under his breath.

Mrs. Thorup walked over, glared at Mrs. Hummel, then gently pried Noel's fingers loose from Macy's dress. Noel screamed even louder and grabbed frantically for her sister. The instant Macy was free of Noel's grasp, Irene pulled her away and pushed her toward the judge's chambers as the little girl, restrained by her father, screamed and swung her arms wildly. "Let me go! Let me go! I want Macy! I want Macy!"

Macy was still whimpering when they got to the door. Irene Hummel dug her fingernails into Macy's shoulder. "Stop crying."

As Macy entered the mahogany-paneled room, her sadness quickly turned to fear. The hearing wasn't held in a courtroom, but in the more private judge's chambers. The judge didn't wear a robe, just a crisp white shirt with a bright blue necktie with yellow and red sailboats. He looked like a kind man, with pictures of his own children and grandchildren strategically placed around his office. He smiled pleasantly at Macy and she could tell he liked kids. He'll understand, she thought. *If she got a chance to tell her story.*

Mrs. Hummel sat close behind her, her knees touching the back of Macy's chair.

The judge looked over his desk at her, softly tapping his brass pen on the leather desk pad, "Hello, Macy."

"Hi," she said timidly. Her fear escalated. She wanted to hide. She wanted her sister back.

The judge leaned forward, his gaze fixed only on her. "Do you know why you're here?"

Under the pressure of his dark eyes she just nodded.

"We are here because the Hummel family would like to adopt you into their family. Do you know what 'adoption' means?"

It means you have to go someplace you don't want to, Macy thought. Again she nodded. The ambient sounds of the room grew loud and drowned out everything else—the brass, glass-domed clock on the shelf, the growling of Mrs. Hummel's stomach—the judge was speaking and she heard words here and there like the tuning of a radio.

"Do you know . . . change your last name? . . . no longer . . . Macy Wood . . . Hummel?"

Then Macy didn't hear him anymore at all. The voice became a drone of authority that pinned her down like gravity. Her eyes opened wider, and the largeness of the moment swallowed her in, and she clutched her chair. Then abruptly everything stopped. Everyone was looking at her.

"Is this okay?" the judge asked gently. He nodded as he spoke and Macy, wide-eyed and trembling, imitated his motion. Didn't he know she was afraid? Couldn't he see the Hummels were bad people?

As quickly as it began, it was over. There were congratulations and smiles. Everyone seemed happy. As Macy walked out, she saw her sister. She was eating a sucker and facing away from the door.

"Sissy."

Noel turned, and Mrs. Thorup quickly put her arm around her to restrain her. Noel began to cry again. "Don't go 'way."

Macy's lip quivered. "Where's your heart, Sissy?"

"Macy," Noel cried. She strained against Mrs. Thorup's grasp. "Let me go!"

"Sissy," Macy repeated. "Where's your heart?"

Noel stopped struggling and put her hand over her chest.

"Keep me there," Macy said.

Noel's soon-to-be father lifted her and carried her into the room and Macy shuffled out with the rest of the Hummels. Macy knew she would never see her Sissy again.

The six Hummels went out for ice cream to celebrate. Macy had a single scoop of mint chocolate chip.

CHAPTER
Eight

There is no amount of compassion or common sense that can't be extinguished by government bureaucracy.

✦ MARK SMART'S DIARY ✦

It had been more than five years since Macy had talked to anyone from the state. The last caseworker she had seen had retired two years earlier, and the woman at the DCFS office referred her to the woman who had taken most of her cases, a middle-aged woman named Andrea Bellamy.

Macy had dressed up for the meeting. She wore an outfit she had borrowed from her roommate, a matching pink silk skirt and jacket with a white pleated blouse. She wanted the caseworker to know that where the state had failed she'd succeeded. She even carried a purse—for her, a symbol of respectability and stability.

✦

The caseworker was a heavyset woman with frosted hair, heavy makeup and bright eyes. She greeted Macy in the lobby. "Hi, I'm Andrea."

"I'm Macy. Nice to meet you."

"Likewise," she said. "Please follow me."

Andrea led her back past a jungle of fabric-padded cubicles to a small conference room. She directed Macy to a chair, then sat down across from her, setting a large folder on the table between them. In the overcrowded schedule of a caseworker there was seldom time for formalities, and Andrea Bellamy quickly launched into the business at hand. "I looked up your file yesterday. I had a little trouble finding it with your name change."

"Yes, ma'am."

"According to your record, you were adopted at the age of eight by Dick and Irene Hummel. Your little sister was adopted by another family on the same day."

"That's right. I just need to know where she is."

The woman looked at her stoically. "I'd like to help you with that but unfortunately her file was ordered sealed by the judge."

Macy looked at her quizzically. "Sealed?"

"It means I can't give you any information about her without a court order."

"How do I get one of those?"

"In a case like this you probably can't."

"What do you mean?"

"In the seven years I've been here, I've never seen it happen."

"But don't I have a right to see my sister?"

"That right is negated by her and her adopted parents' right to privacy."

"Why would my sister want privacy from me?"

The woman didn't answer.

"Could you tell me her name?"

"You don't remember her name?"

Macy shook her head. "I've forgotten."

"I'm sorry, but I can't tell you anything."

Macy rested her head in the palm of her hand. "Is there any way around this?"

"Only if your sister decides that she wants to see you and makes a formal request. I now have your phone number and address, so I'll contact you if that happens."

"But she might not even remember me. She was only four when we were separated."

The woman looked at Macy sympathetically. "I'm really sorry. I wish I could be of more help, but it's the law."

Macy's voice was sharp with anger. "But she's my sister. We had no choice . . ."

Macy looked into the woman's eyes. "How can complete strangers make that decision for us?"

Again the woman didn't answer.

"Do you think it's fair?"

"No, I don't. But we're bound by the law, and sometimes the law and *'fair'* are two different things."

After a moment Macy pointed to the folder between them. "Can I see my file?"

"I can't show it to you either."

"I can't see my own file?"

"I'm afraid not. There's information in here about your biological parents and it's been sealed as well."

"Then I have no place to go."

"I'm afraid not."

Macy wavered between crying and raging. "What if someone told you that you couldn't ever see your family again?"

"I didn't say it was fair, Macy. Just that it's the law."

"It's a bad law. Can't you give me any help? This is *my* life—she's my *sister.*"

The woman just looked at her. "I wish I could help you. I really do."

Macy's eyes filled. Suddenly a page came

over the office phone system. "Andrea Bellamy, you have a call on line five."

"I need to get that," Andrea said apologetically. She glanced over at the phone in
the corner of the room, then back at Macy.
Her expression became thoughtful. "I think
I'll take that call back in my office." Her eyes
fell on the folder between them. Macy
looked at the folder, then up into her eyes
and understood.

"I'll probably be five minutes."

"You wouldn't have a pen and paper,
would you?"

Andrea pulled a plastic pen from her
valise and handed it to her. "There's a note
pad by the phone. She walked to the door,
leaving Macy staring at the folder on the
desk. She turned back once more. "Five
minutes."

"Thank you," Macy said.

"For what?" Andrea Bellamy replied.
"Like I said, I can't help you." She shut the
door behind herself.

Macy grabbed the file and began thumb-
ing through it. It was half an inch thick
and contained a complete record of each of
her placements. There was a psychological
profile of her, which she didn't have time to

read so she folded it and put it in her purse. She found a report with her father's name and an address. She retrieved the notepad and copied down her father's information.

By the time Andrea returned, Macy was on her way out of the building.

CHAPTER
Nine

I have puzzled over the phrase "The road to hell is paved with good intentions." Does that mean people intend well but never actually do it? Or that they do good things with bad results? I suppose it doesn't matter much. Either way the right thing doesn't get done.

✦ MARK SMART'S DIARY ✦

AUGUST 17, 1978

Every other month Irene Hummel had her hair done by Sadie, a cousin of hers who lived an hour south in the small town of Nephi. Macy looked forward to those days, as she was always dropped off at her Aunt Stephanie's. Macy liked it there. Aunt Stephanie lived in the country. She had a secret garden and a large gray cat named Tabitha. Aunt Stephanie made her honey and butter sandwiches and Campbell's tomato soup with lots of saltine crackers. She kept Twinkies in the freezer, and in the afternoon they'd take one out and eat it with the filling still cold. She was the only one who still called her Macy. Macy McGracy.

Things had been getting steadily worse at the Hummel house for Macy. One Saturday afternoon, Mr. Hummel packed his bags and left for good. Not long after, Mrs. Hummel started hitting Macy on nearly a daily basis. That morning, as Macy sat quietly in the back seat of the car on the way to Aunt Stephanie's, a thought crossed her mind. Maybe if she told Aunt Stephanie about Mrs. Hummel, she'd invite her to live with her. It seemed reasonable. Aunt Stephanie always told her how much she liked having her around. Still, it took Macy all day to get the courage to tell her. Her Aunt was sitting in the parlor tying a quilt when Macy sauntered into the room. She looked up and smiled.

"What are you up to, dearie?"

"Nothing."

She continued working on the quilt. Suddenly Macy blurted out, "Mrs. Hummel hits me."

Aunt Stephanie turned and looked at her. "What's that, sweetie?"

"Mrs. Hummel hits me."

"Oh, your mom would never hit you. She probably spanks you sometimes."

"She hits me every day. Sometimes in my face."

Aunt Stephanie stopped tying and looked at her. "Is that so?"

Macy nodded, "Uh-huh."

For a moment she seemed unsure of

what to say. "Well then I'll just have to talk to her."

Macy's blood went cold. "Please don't tell her."

"If she's hitting you, someone's got to talk to her. We can't have that kind of nonsense going on. Now run along while I call."

Macy walked from the room, nearly paralyzed with fear. She desperately regretted telling her aunt.

Three hours later Mrs. Hummel arrived to pick her up.

"Nightie night, Macy McGracy," Aunt Stephanie said as she walked from the house. "Come back soon."

"Good night," Macy said.

Macy climbed into the car as somber as a condemned man climbing the gallows. She was afraid to look at Mrs. Hummel, but Mrs. Hummel acted like nothing was wrong. *Maybe Aunt Stephanie forgot to call,* Macy hoped. It was dark when they pulled into their driveway. Macy walked into the house, followed by Mrs. Hummel.

As soon as the front door shut, a hand caught Macy across the back of her head. "So I hit you?" she said.

Macy knew better than to answer. She

backed up against a wall and stared at her mother in fear.

"I spank you for being naughty. It's your fault. It's your fault for being such an awful girl. We never should have brought you into this family. It's been nothing but trouble since you came here." She slapped a hand across the top of Macy's head. "Dick left because of you. Because of all the trouble you cause."

Macy held still, careful to do nothing that might add fuel to the woman's ferocity.

"I *hit* you, you brat? You don't know what hitting is. *This* is hitting." She smacked Macy across the side of the face and Macy fell back against the wall. A thin trickle of blood fell down her nose to her chin. "And this. And this . . ."

Macy did her best to protect herself from the barrage of blows, but they were too fast, and too random. The beating went on for another five minutes until Mrs. Hummel had exhausted herself and stood over her, panting, her eyes wild and cruel. Macy slumped down on the floor, covering herself the best she could and afraid to look Mrs. Hummel in the eyes. She whimpered softly, "I'm sorry."

"Yeah, you're sorry now." Mrs. Hummel's

coup de grâce was a kick to Macy's side, but it wasn't hard. She hadn't much strength left.

"You stupid brat. If you ever tell anyone else that I hit you, they'll tell me just like Stephanie did. Then I'll really show you what hitting is."

Macy sniffed. "I won't say anything."

"I say you won't! And the dishes better be done when I get up in the morning."

She swaggered off down the corridor. After her bedroom door slammed shut, Macy went to the bathroom and got some toilet paper and held it to her nose until the bleeding stopped. Then she went to the kitchen and began to wash the dishes.

✦

Macy didn't go back to school for a week, not until her black eye and bruises had faded. Mrs. Hummel told the school that Macy had the flu. The next time Macy saw her aunt, she looked different to her. She was no longer Twinkies and honey sandwiches. She was now part of Mrs. Hummel and just like the rest of her world—a wobbly rope bridge over a raging river.

Her aunt was doing the dishes when she casually asked if Irene ever hit her anymore.

"No, ma'am," Macy said quickly. A proud smile crossed her aunt's face.

"See, isn't it good to just get these things out in the open? People are good at heart. It's all about communication."

Macy never again told anyone else what Mrs. Hummel did to her.

CHAPTER

Ten

C. S. Lewis said it best, "I like bats more than bureaucrats."

✦ MARK SMART'S DIARY ✦

On the way home from work, I stopped at a 7-Eleven to use the pay phone and called Macy. Before I could say anything she blurted out, "They separated us on purpose."

"Who did?"

"The state."

"That's what they told you?"

"No, they couldn't tell me anything. But in my state file there was a psychological profile on me. Some social worker wrote that I was my sister's primary caregiver, and he thought if we stayed together it *might* hurt her chances of bonding in a traditional family setting. He therefore, and I quote, 'strongly recommends that the sisters be separated and sent to different homes.'

"Can you believe that? They separated us because I loved her and was taking care of her!"

"That's real genius," I said sarcastically. "So did you find out where she lives?"

"No. But I got my father's address. He should know where she lives."

"I'd think so," I said.

"I'm going to drive out to his house."

She said this casually, as if seeing her father was something she did on a regular basis.

"How long has it been since you saw your father?"

"Fourteen years."

"How do you feel about seeing him?" I asked.

"I'm a little nervous."

"Do you want me to go with you?"

"Would you?"

"Of course. When do you want to go?"

"I was thinking first thing tomorrow. Maybe around nine."

"I'll pick you up."

"Great. Oh, and Jo will be there. You two can finally meet. Let me give you my address."

I scribbled it down. "I'll see you tomorrow," I said.

"Tomorrow," she said. "Tomorrow my world changes."

CHAPTER
Eleven

I believe that whatever good or evil we do in this life eventually comes back to us. But in the case of rampant evil, it brings its friends.

✦ MARK SMART'S DIARY ✦

JUNE 16, 1981

It was a year and a half after her husband left when Mrs. Hummel took to her bed. She stayed in her room for days at a time, the blinds drawn, occasionally summoning one of the kids to her side to bring her food. For the most part, Bart, Ron and Sheryl ignored her, embracing her absence as an opportunity for pleasant anarchy. Ironically, only Macy, who was now fifteen, felt sorry for her. She did her best to keep the house in order, sometimes using her own money, earned by babysitting, to buy groceries.

One night Macy's best friend, Tracy, followed her home. She stood outside the door while Macy walked into Mrs. Hummel's darkened room.

"Where have you been?" Mrs. Hummel growled. "I've been calling for you for hours. I've practically lost my voice."

"I could only wish," Macy mumbled.

"What?"

"Nothing. I just got home. I went grocery shopping. We were out of milk and cereal."

"Where's Sheryl?"

"I don't know." Macy actually did. She had seen her down the street, smoking with a group of boys.

"Get over here."

Macy walked to her side. Irene lunged at her in an effort to hit her, but her swing was sufficiently slow that she missed. Macy was now bigger and stronger than Mrs. Hummel and could have easily retaliated but never did.

"You find your sister. It's your fault she's not around."

Macy turned from her.

"Don't you walk out on me! Don't you walk out on me!"

Macy walked out of the room. Outside in the hallway her friend Tracy was seething. "I'm going to give that witch a piece of my mind."

"No, you're not. Let's just get out of here." Macy led her friend out to the living room.

"Why do you put up with that?"

"She's just sick."

"She's sick in the head. Even my mom

says so. The woman's a nutcase." Tracy exhaled in frustration. "Listen, Mace, I can't be your friend anymore and watch what goes on here."

"Yeah, well what am I supposed to do about it?"

"My mom says you can live at our place for as long as you need."

Macy glanced back at the room. After a moment she said, "I'll think about it."

"There's nothing to think about. Get your things right now."

"I don't know."

"It's me or the witch. I'm not going to watch this anymore." Tracy walked to the front door. As she turned the handle, she looked back once more. "Are you coming?"

"Wait," Macy said.

Tracy's voice was calm but emotional. "I mean it, Mace. If you won't let me help you, then I'm leaving."

She glanced down the dark corridor, then back at her friend. "Give me a minute to pack."

It took Macy less than ten minutes to collect her things. She threw everything into a canvas duffel except one small box that she carried separately.

"What's in the box?" Tracy asked.

"It's my Christmas ornament. My father gave it to me the day they took me away."

"May I see it?"

"Yeah. But be careful." Macy handed over the box as gingerly as if it held a Fabergé egg.

Tracy examined it. "Wow. I'm surprised it's still in one piece in this house."

"I keep it hidden. I only take it out on Christmas Day."

"It's beautiful." She handed back the box. "Let's blow this dump."

Macy followed Tracy out of the house, quietly closing the door behind her.

CHAPTER
Twelve

Today I met Macy's best friend, Joette. From Macy's description I fully expected wings and a halo, not a Utah Jazz sweatshirt and a White Sox baseball cap.

✦MARK SMART'S DIARY✦

I looked outside and shook my head. It was snowing again. It was only November and I was already sick of the snow and the cold. It would have been difficult to find Macy's home with the mailboxes and curbs covered with snow, but Macy had instructed me to look for the duplex with the most Christmas decorations. It was easy to find. I recognized Macy's car in the driveway and I pulled in behind her.

The door was decorated with a Christmas wreath. I rang the bell, and a petite woman in her early forties wearing a sweatshirt and a White Sox baseball cap opened the door. Her red ponytail was pulled through the back of the hat.

"You must be Mark."

"I am."

"I'm Joette. Come in." She looked past me. "Ah, it's snowing again."

I stepped inside. "Yeah, you get a lot of snow here in Utah."

"Especially this year." She shut the door behind me.

The living room was small and looked lived in, but it was neat and well cared for. It smelled pleasant, like one of those scented candles—nutmeg and cinnamon. There were pictures around the home, mostly black-and-white photographs: like Ansel Adams landscapes. In the far corner was a picture of Jesus, and beneath it, on a dark maple stand, was a Bible. Peculiarly, a framed *Wizard of Oz* movie poster hung above the fireplace.

The house was decorated for Christmas. There were two crèches displayed separately on the end tables at each end of the sofa: one carved of olive wood, the other pastel porcelain. Across the lid of an upright piano a mass of pink angel hair flowed between three large glass candleholders.

"Have a seat."

I sat down at the sofa, and she sat down on the opposite end, her hands folded in her lap. "It's nice to finally meet you," she said. "Macy's told me a little about you."

"And you still let me in?"

"We always take in strays," she said smiling. Her expression changed to one of concern. "I'm sorry to hear about your mother."

"Thank you."

"It's a hard thing. I lost my mother when I was in high school. I still miss her." She sighed and noticeably changed the topic. "So Macy says you're from Alabama."

"Yes, ma'am."

"You certainly are. No one in Utah says 'ma'am.' Except Macy. But you can call me Joette. Or Jo. That's what Macy calls me."

"Yes, ma'am," I said instinctively, and she grinned.

"Sorry."

"No, I quite like it. So the two of you are off on an adventure today."

"I think so."

"I'm glad you're going with her. This isn't an easy thing for Macy to do alone."

Macy walked into the room. She was nicely dressed in slacks and a suede jacket, and she had clearly spent extra time on her hair and makeup. I guessed that since she hadn't seen her father in fourteen years she wanted to make a good impression. "Hi."

I stood. "Hi. You look nice."

"Thanks." She turned to Joette. "I should be back before work. Don't worry about dinner."

"Okay. Good luck." Macy kissed her.

"It was nice meeting you," I said.

"Likewise. I hope I see more of you."

"Thank you. Me too."

She followed us to the door and stood there as we walked to the car. I opened the car door for Macy, then walked around.

When I climbed in, Macy said, "That was a good thing."

"What?"

"Opening the door for me. Joette was watching. She's big on boys opening car doors."

"Glad to get off on the right foot." I started the car.

"So, what did you guys talk about?"

"Nothing much. She told me she was sorry about my mother."

"Jo lost her mother when she was in high school."

"That's what she said." I put the car in reverse and paused. "Where to?"

"It's in Magna. Do you know where that is?"

"It's west somewhere."

"Just get on Twenty-First South and head toward the Oquirrh Mountains."

I pulled out of the driveway and started

off. After a few miles I said, "Tell me about Joette."

Macy smiled. "Jo's my angel. She's the most beautiful soul I've ever met."

"So you like her then?"

Her smile broadened. "Like chocolate."

"That *is* love."

"When I first moved in with her, Jo worked until two or three in the morning, but I was off before midnight. So instead of going to bed, I would stay up and clean the house and vacuum and do the washing and ironing. After about two weeks I woke one morning and Jo was sitting on the edge of my bed. She said, 'We need to talk.' Of course I assumed I'd done something wrong. She said, 'It's about the cleaning.' I said, 'I can do better.' She just looked at me, and then she said something I'll never forget. She said, 'Macy. You don't have to be perfect to live here or to make me love you.' That was it. She got up and left. I started to cry. It was the first time I had ever felt unconditional love." Her eyes moistened. "I'd take a bullet for her."

"You're lucky to have someone to love like that," I said.

"I know. I don't take it for granted. What's

scary is I almost lost her a few years back. She had cancer in her eye. Thank goodness the cancer went into remission. It's been almost three years." She took a deep breath. "I'm so grateful. I couldn't live without her."

"What's with the *Wizard of Oz* poster?"

She chuckled. "You noticed. Joette's a *Wizard of Oz* maniac. I think she believes that everything you need to know about life can be learned from *The Wizard of Oz.* That poster was autographed by Bert Lahr."

"Who's that?"

"He played the Cowardly Lion in the movie."

I nodded. "Impressive."

Macy spoke less the farther west we traveled. Magna is an old copper-mining town, its main street largely abandoned and dying. Macy stared at the buildings as we passed them, and I wondered how much she remembered from her childhood. She suddenly pointed.

"I remember walking to that store. We lived on that street up ahead, by the old theater."

I turned at the corner where a battered yellow theater marquee overhung the street. What letters remained partially spelled the title of some forgotten movie from a previous decade, like an interrupted game of hangman. I drove slowly, straining at addresses on the homes or mailboxes or where snow didn't cover the curbs. Three blocks later Macy said in a voice low with disappointment, "I think that's it."

I stopped the car and checked the address she'd written down. It was the right house number but the place was clearly abandoned. The windows were boarded over with large sheets of plywood spray-painted NO TRESPASSING. The yard was surrounded with a waist-high chain-link fence. The snow was piled in high drifts on the west side, and weeds and thistles peeked out here and there from the snow. We climbed out of the car. Macy opened the gate, then stepped up through the snow to the house, her feet sinking into the white up to her thighs. She climbed onto the porch and peered through the boards into the house. I followed her up and stood next to her. She said to me, "I want to go inside."

I checked the front door but it was locked. I looked around to see if anyone was watching us. I could see no one around, so I grabbed the corner of the plywood sheet nailed over the north window and pried it off. I had to throw all my weight against it, and it fell back on the porch with a loud crash. I looked at Macy. "I'll get the door for you."

I climbed inside. The house was dark; I flipped on the light switch to no effect and realized what a stupid thing that was. I was glad Macy hadn't seen me. There was a musty, pungent smell of mold from rotting carpet and drywall.

I unbolted the front door. Macy walked inside and stood in the center of the living room and looked around. We weren't the home's first trespassers. There was a man-made rat's nest in the corner strewn with empty beer bottles and cigarette stubs. There was graffiti on the wall. Macy didn't seem to notice any of it. She wandered quietly from room to room with me in tow.

"This is like a dream of a dream," she said. "It seemed so much bigger back then." She started down into the basement, but it was flooded with several feet of water. She descended to the lowest stair possible, looked around, then came back up.

"Everything's gone," she said sadly. "How will I find him now?"

I frowned. "I'm sorry," I said.

She walked out the front door. I locked the deadbolt and was climbing back out the window when someone shouted. "What are you doing in there?! The sign says NO TRESPASSING!"

An elderly black woman with silver hair stood on the sidewalk in front of the house. She was nearly as broad as she was high, and wore a bright red wool coat with faux fur collar and black buttons as big as sand dollars, and black rubber galoshes. A sheer scarf was knotted over her head, and a small plastic shopping bag was draped over the crook of one arm. A silver-haired Yorkshire terrier pulled at the leash she held, sniffing around in the snow.

Macy was feeling bad enough, I thought, without an altercation with some cranky old lady. "We're just leaving," I said. I took Macy's arm and walked her down the steps. The woman just stood there staring at us.

"They should've torn that place down years ago. Place is a magnet for hobos and runaways. Which are you?"

"Excuse me?" Macy said.

"Which are you, hobos or runaways?"

Macy stopped. "We're neither," she said gently.

"Someday someone's gonna set fire to that place and the whole neighborhood's gonna go up in flames. Not that anyone would mind that much."

"Let's go," I said, tugging at Macy's arm.

Macy didn't move. Instead she stepped back toward the woman. "I was looking for someone who used to live here."

"No one's lived there more than ten years, honey." Then the woman strained to look at her. "Come closer."

To my surprise Macy walked over to her. When she was within arm's reach, the woman squinted and examined her more closely. Then she slowly reached out and touched Macy's cheek. A smile broke across the wrinkled face. "Well, now, you're just all grown up now, aren't you, little Macy?"

Macy looked at her in astonishment. "How do you know my name?"

"Why would I forget that?"

"Do I know you?"

"You did. You used to play at my house almost every day." She gazed into her face as if waiting for her to remember. "We'd get the old player piano going."

Macy looked down. "I remember a piano. I'd play at your house?"

"Almost every day, especially when your mama was so sick. You and your sister would come over and ask me for chocolate. I used to have them Brach's stars in the plastic sacks."

"You know my sister?"

"I should hope so. Well as I know you."

"Do you know my sister's name?"

The woman just looked at her. "My stars, what have they done to you?" She tugged on the dog's leash. "You come home with me. We have some catching up to do."

The old lady turned and looked at me. "I know I don't know *you.*"

"I'm a friend of Macy's," I said.

She extended the grocery bag to me. "Well, friend, would you mind carrying my bag? I'm an old lady."

I took the sack from her. "No problem."

She turned to her dog. "C'mon, Fred, let's you and I take Macy home."

CHAPTER

Thirteen

Big Day. We learned Macy's sister's name. It was hanging from her Christmas tree all along.

✦ MARK SMART'S DIARY ✦

The woman lived just three houses down from Macy's old home in a red brick house with cloth awnings that looked altogether out of place in a neighborhood where prefab houses covered in aluminum siding were the norm. She had lived in the same home for fifty-seven of her eighty-two years of life, she told us.

With some effort she climbed the seven steps of the concrete porch; we followed after her. She brought a tangle of keys from her coat pocket, unlocked the door and we all went inside.

She crouched down and unleashed her dog, then stood. "I'll take the milk now."

I handed her the bag, and she hobbled off to the kitchen, leaving Macy and me alone in the living room. The front room was rectangular, the floor covered with gold shag carpet, the walls coated with faux gold-leafed wallpaper yellowed with age, especially near the windows. The furniture looked like it had been bought in the fifties, and the house smelled of lilac air freshener. On one of the walls was a faded mural of Hawaii. Mounted on the opposite wall was a display of Wedgwood plates above an antique player piano, a leviathan of an instrument with wood cabinetry set in a herringbone pattern.

In one corner of the room was a squat artificial Christmas tree with a single strand of lights hung haphazardly across it. In the opposite corner of the living room was a three-stepped étagère of burled walnut adorned with porcelain figurines. Macy walked over to it and squatted down to examine the dolls. I sat down on the couch and watched her.

"You came on a good day," the woman said from the other room. "I'm going to be hand-dipping my Christmas chocolates. Cordials and haystacks." She came back into the room carrying a plate of cookies. "Haven't changed much, have you, girl?"

Macy turned to her. "Excuse me?"

"You loved those dolls. Always went right to them."

She cocked her head. "I remember these."

"See that one with the broken arm?"

"Yes."

"You did that. Well, maybe Noel did it and you took the blame for it. Never got the truth out of you; you were always looking out for her."

"Noel. That's her name," she said as if it had just been pulled from somewhere deep in her mind. "It's on my Christmas ornament."

"Christina Noel. Born Christmas Day."

"I always felt something whenever I heard that song," Macy said," 'The First Noel.' "

"I always sang that to her when you came over, even in the summer. You both were the cutest little things. You made quite a sight coming up the walk hand in hand. I used to tell you, you should sue the county for building the sidewalk so close to your rear." She laughed.

"I used to sing to you too. Your favorite song was 'You're a little bit of honey that the bees ain't found.' And you liked that song from *Mary Poppins,* 'Feed the birds, tuppence a bag . . . ' "

The woman's voice was irregular and scratchy like an old vinyl record, but it washed over Macy like a warm wave. "I used to have a voice," she continued.

"I remember," Macy said.

"Had a trio with my sisters. We were popular back then. Sang at the opening of St. Mark's Hospital. Course I had looks too, and you can see where that got me."

She held out the plate. "Ginger snap?"

Macy took one. "I love ginger snaps," she said.

"I know. Take two."

Macy took another, then the woman offered the plate to me and I took one. Then she took a cookie for herself. "I used to tell you that if you ate one more ginger snap you'd turn into one. You believed me too. You'd puzzle over that like it might be a good thing."

Macy said hesitantly, "I'm sorry, but I don't remember your name."

"You just called me Nanna. My name's Bonnie Foster."

"Bonnie Foster," Macy repeated. "Did you know my mother well?"

"You don't think your mother would just send you off to a stranger's house, do you?" She pushed herself up by her knees. "Just a minute." She left the room, and we could hear her rooting through the hall closet. She returned carrying an old shoe box. "Want to see a picture of her?"

"You have pictures of us?"

"Course I do. All of you. Even your father."

Bonnie set the box on the coffee table in front of us. Macy reached for the pictures. The first photo was of two little girls posing in Easter dresses.

"That's me and Noel?"

Bonnie smiled. "Cuter than a bug's ears."

"You look alike," I said.

"Oh yes," Bonnie said. "The two of you could've been twins if it wasn't for the age."

Macy went through several other pictures of her and her sister. In one of them the children sat on a woman's lap.

"That's my mother," Macy said softly.

Bonnie looked over. "Your dear mother."

"She was beautiful."

"Heavens, yes. She was beautiful inside too. Your mother was a saint."

Macy looked at her quizzically. "A saint?"

"It's a sin to counsel the Lord, but I don't know why He always takes His best when we need them so badly down here. There He's got all those martyrs and saints, and when we get one of them down here it's like

He just wants them back. He should have taken your father." She quickly turned away. "I shouldn't have said that. Now I've sinned twice. I'll be keeping Father Lapina busy at confessional this Sunday."

I thought of my own situation and how many times in the last few weeks I'd thought the very same thing, that it should have been my father.

Macy set down the picture. "You said my mother was sick?"

"She had cancer of the lung."

"Cancer? You mean she didn't die from drinking?"

"Your mama? Heavens no! I don't think she touched a drop in all her life. Where'd you get that fool idea?"

"Irene Hummel told me."

"And who's Irene Hummel?"

"The woman who adopted me."

Bonnie shook her head. "Now I *know* that's a sin, talking about your mother that way. Your mother was an angel if ever there was one on this earth."

"What about my father?"

Her expression hardened. "That man's a different story." She shuffled through the pictures. "There he is." The photograph

showed a thin man, leaning against a mo-
torcycle, a cigarette dangling from his lip.
"That man was the bane of her existence.
He was her only hope of keeping the family
together. But he let her down. He let all of
you down."

"Why'd she marry him?" I asked, seeing
another similarity with my parents.

"Question I couldn't figure is why she
didn't leave him. But then, love isn't reasonable."

Macy finally asked the question she'd
been waiting to ask. "Do you know where
Noel is?"

"No. Wish I did. One day they just came
and took her. I never saw her again. But I'm
sure someone at the state could tell you."

"Macy just shook her head. They've
sealed all our records."

"Why would they do that?"

"They say they wanted privacy."

"Who's 'they'?"

"My sister and her new family."

"That doesn't make any sense."

"I didn't think so either. I guess my best
bet is still to find my father. Do you know
where he is?"

Bonnie frowned. "He lost the house a year or two after you all left."

"Do you know where he moved to?"

"No. If he hasn't died." She noticed the look of distress on Macy's face. "But I doubt it. I read the obituaries every day and I haven't seen him there."

"He's not in the phone book," Macy said. "If he's as bad as you say, he might not even remember who took her."

"Things will work out," Bonnie said. "Remember the Psalms: Be still and know that I am God. That means God is at the helm. It's right there in the Good Book. Look how we found each other." She looked into Macy's face. "It's so good to see you again."

"It's good to see you again," Macy said.

"Now, tell me about this boy."

"Mark's a friend of mine. He's from Alabama."

"My old neighborhood. You're a long way from home."

"Yes, ma'am, I am."

"Where 'bout in Alabama?"

"Huntsville."

"My people are from Montgomery." She

smiled and patted Macy's thigh. "I'd love to have you both for Sunday dinner."

"That would be nice." She turned to me. "Are you busy, Mark?"

Her question was only a formality. "No, I'm free."

"I have church until one o'clock," Bonnie said. "Would dinner at two be okay?"

"Two's great," Macy said.

Bonnie and Macy exchanged phone numbers, and then we got up to leave. The dog, Fred, jumped up and ran around us, barking frantically.

"Hush up, Fred," Bonnie said. "Hush."

We stopped at the door. "What can I bring for dinner?" Macy asked.

"Just yourself. And this boyfriend of yours."

Macy didn't correct her. "Then we'll see you Sunday."

"Wait. You never left without a kiss for Nanna."

Macy smiled, "Sorry, I forgot." She kissed the old woman's cheek.

"You can kiss me too," she said to me.

I kissed her on the other cheek.

"See you Sunday—come hungry."

When we got back into the car, Macy

started to cry and didn't stop until we were halfway home.

When we were back in Salt Lake, I asked Macy, "Want to get some lunch?"

"No. Not unless you do."

"I'm okay."

She looked back out the window.

"Are you okay?"

"What if I never find her?"

"You'll find her. It will work out."

"How can you be sure?"

"It's like Bonnie said: fate plays a hand in these things. I mean, look how we found Bonnie. What were the odds of that?"

"You're right." A moment later she said, "One of our regulars at the Hut is a private eye. I wonder if he'd help look for my dad."

"I'm sure he would. I bet this kind of stuff is easy for him."

She smiled. "You know, I *am* kind of hungry."

We stopped at a McDonald's for fish sandwiches. An hour later I dropped Macy off at home. "Do you want to come in?" she asked.

"I need to get to work. I'm already late."

"I work tonight too." She leaned over and

kissed me on the cheek. "Thanks for coming with me."

"Anytime. I'll call you tomorrow."

"Okay, have fun at work." She ran into the house, and I drove to work wishing that I didn't have to leave her and wondering where our journey would take us next.

CHAPTER

Fourteen

Sometimes you can't go home again.

✦MARK SMART'S DIARY✦

When I returned home from work, I found a note my landlord had pushed under my apartment door. It read in hurried scrawl, "Call your Aunt Marge collect, *no matter the hour.*" A phone number with a Huntsville area code was written beneath. Aunt Marge was my mother's only sister and one of the three women in the car accident with my mother. I was surprised to hear from her and was worried by the note's urgent tone.

I put the note in my pocket, walked outside and down the street to the corner 7-Eleven's outside pay phone. The headset was cold against my face. I asked the operator to make the call. On the fourth ring, a sleepy voice answered. "Mark?"

"I have a collect call from Mark Smart," the operator said. "Will you accept the charges?"

"Of course."

"Go ahead, sir."

"Aunt Marge," I said.

"Oh, Mark, I'm so glad you called."

"I'm sorry to call so late. I just got off work and got your message. Is something wrong?"

"Nothing new. I've just been so worried about you."

I was relieved to hear there was no bad news.

"Are you back in school?"

"Not yet. I'm saving for it. But it's going to take a while."

"Can I help?"

I knew she meant it, but I could never in good conscience accept money from her. She had been divorced eight years earlier, and with four children and minimal child support, her life had been a constant financial struggle. "Thanks, Aunt Marge, but I'll get by."

"Mark, I promised your mother that I would look after you. When are you coming home?"

"I don't really have any plans to come back."

"But you'll be home for Christmas?"

I hesitated. "I don't know."

"What do you mean?"

"There's really no reason to come back."

"What about your dad?"

This question was easier. "The last time I spoke to Stu, he told me not to come home."

She was quiet a moment. "I know. He told me. He regrets saying it."

In twenty-one years I had never heard Stu apologize for or retract anything. "Stu told you that he regrets saying it?"

"In so many words."

I figured as much. "Well, he seemed pretty sure about it when he said it to me."

"He was just in a bad way. He's having a hard time."

"He can join the club. We've got jackets."

She was taken aback by my sarcasm. "Mark, you're not the only one suffering. Alice was his wife, and she was my sister and best friend."

"I'm sorry, Aunt Marge. I didn't mean to be disrespectful. I appreciate your concern. It's just . . . there's really nothing back in Huntsville for me. Stu and I just don't get along."

She was silent for what seemed like a long time. "You know, Mark, people aren't always who they seem to be."

"You can't tell me that Stu's a good father."

"I'm telling you that you don't really know him."

"With all due respect, I think I know my father."

"You know what you know. But you don't know the whole story."

"What story?"

"Your parents' story."

"Then tell me."

"It's not mine to tell. But someday you'll understand. Hopefully it won't be too late. For your sake, and your father's."

I didn't know what to say. I couldn't imagine any scenario that could change how I felt about him. After a moment I said, "Can I ask you something?"

"Of course."

"You were with my mother in the accident?"

"Yes."

"Will you tell me what happened?"

I had asked a difficult thing, for both of us, and she paused to gather herself. "I really didn't want to do this over the telephone."

I sat down on the cold concrete, the

metal-wrapped phone cord stretched taut. "I know. I just need to know."

She was quiet for another moment, then her voice came more softly: "Alright. You know we ladies get together every month. We went to the Sandpiper for lunch. On the way home it started raining, hard. The wipers could barely keep up. Your mother was driving. We weren't even going very fast, but suddenly there was a truck stopped in front of us. Your mother swerved to miss it and we went off the road and flipped over an embankment. The car rolled three times until it struck a tree and stopped upside down. We hit on your mother's door."

I began to cry. I was afraid to ask the next question but I had to know. "Was she killed instantly?"

"No. We tried to help her, but we couldn't get her out of her seat belt." Her voice started to tremble with emotion. "I held her while we waited for help. She bled to death before the paramedics arrived."

It was a moment before I could speak. "Was she in a lot of pain?"

"She didn't complain of it. But she was in shock."

I wiped back my cheek with the back of my hand. "Did she say anything?"

"Yes. She wanted me to tell you that she loves you with all of her heart and always will. And that she'll be watching over you."

I wiped my eyes. After a moment I asked, "Did she say anything else?"

"Yes. But it wasn't for you."

"Who was it for?"

"Stu."

"Could you tell me what she said?"

She hesitated. "I don't know."

"I'm just trying to hold on to everything I can of her. It would really help me to know what her last thoughts were."

She pondered my request for another moment. "Maybe I should. It might help you. It might help both of you. She wanted me to tell him that she was sorry."

I suppose that I had expected anything but this. Something about it ignited my defenses, turning my grief to anger. "*She* was sorry? For what?"

"You'll have to ask him."

I was speechless. I couldn't comprehend anything that my mother could be sorry about. All I could see was that my father had made her life miserable. All of our lives miserable.

"I'll let you go," she said. "Do you need anything?"

"No."

"Mark, please consider coming home. You can stay with us if you like, but please give him a chance."

After a minute I said, "I'll think about it."

"If you change your mind, just call me. Call me collect, anytime, day or night. I'll pay your airfare."

"Thank you. I'll let you know."

"You still have my phone number?"

"I have it written down."

"Okay. You take care of yourself. I'll check up on you later."

"Thanks for calling, Aunt Marge."

"You're welcome, Mark. I love you."

"I love you too."

I stood and replaced the phone in its cradle. My heart ached as I walked back to my apartment. It was like hearing the news of my mother's death again for the first time. In my mind I played out the last moments of my mother's life. Her brown Impala flying through the air in slow motion. But what stuck with me the most was my mother's last words—her apology to Stu. What could my mother possibly be sorry about? I fell asleep with this on my mind.

C H A P T E R

Fifteen

Macy and I made a real date for tomorrow. The difference in my feelings for the girls I've dated before and Macy is the difference between Labor Day and Christmas.

✦MARK SMART'S DIARY✦

I woke the next morning with what felt like an emotional hangover.

Shortly before noon I went out to call Macy.

"I talked to Tim," she said.

"Who's Tim?"

"He's the private eye I told you about. I saw him last night at work. He did a search for my dad, but he couldn't find him. Tim said it usually means one of two things. Either he's in prison or he's moved out of state. From what Bonnie said, both are pretty likely."

"So should we go out to the prison?"

"I already called. They won't tell you if someone's there or not. It's against the rules."

"It seems like the government is conspiring to keep you from your sister."

"It sure feels like it," she said. "How are things going for you?"

"My aunt called from Alabama. She was

in the car with my mother. I made her tell me the details of the accident."

"Are you okay?"

"It was hard. But I had to know."

"I'm sorry," she said. "What else did she say?"

"She wanted to know when I was coming home. She was pretty upset when I told her that I didn't have any plans to return."

"I can understand that. You're family."

"The weird thing is she was genuinely concerned about my father. She thinks I need to go see him. That's about the last thing I want to do."

Macy thought about this. "It's a little ironic, isn't it? I'm upset that I can't find my father. And you're running from yours."

"I'm not running," I said. "I just don't want to see him."

"Sorry," she said quietly.

I felt stupid for reacting so defensively. "I guess I'm a little sensitive about the whole father thing."

"Understandably."

"Do you want to get together?" I asked.

"Of course. When?"

"When *don't* you work?"

"I can get tomorrow night off."

"May I take you on a date?"

Her voice lightened. "A real date?"

"If that's okay."

"Sure. What do you want to do?"

"I have something in mind. I'll pick you up at six."

"What are we doing?"

"It's a surprise. But dress warm. Really warm."

"Like a parka and boots?"

"Yeah. Like you're going to the North Pole. And don't eat. Oh, and bring a swimsuit."

"A swimsuit and boots. This sounds interesting. All right. I'll see you tomorrow."

"Okay. I'll see you then."

"Can't wait."

CHAPTER
Sixteen

*We went up into the canyons as friends.
We came back down something else.
I'm not sure what, but definitely
something else.*

✦ MARK SMART'S DIARY ✦

The next morning I taught my first guitar lesson. My student was a thirteen-year-old boy who wanted to be a heavy-metal guitarist and kept pounding his guitar like a tom-tom. His mother had picked up one of the flyers from the coffee shop. She dropped him off at my apartment with twenty dollars and the guitar he got for his birthday.

After lunch I drove to a nearby supermarket and bought groceries for our date. It took me nearly an hour to prepare the meal, which was probably more time than I had spent in the kitchen in the last three months. I picked Macy up at six. I took her up Big Cottonwood Canyon near the southeast end of the valley. A third of the way up the canyon, I pulled off the road into a campground.

When we had parked, I took from my trunk a shovel I had borrowed from my landlord, pushed the snow from the closest picnic table, and laid a vinyl tarp across the bench. I then retrieved from my car a bundle of firewood, some newspaper, matches, a plastic water jug and a small red Igloo cooler.

Macy came out of the car and watched as I chopped some of the larger pieces of wood into kindling, then built a teepee and laid the larger wood around it. In less than five minutes we had a roaring fire.

"I'm guessing you were an Eagle Scout," Macy said.

"I was a Life Scout."

"What's that?"

"One badge shy of an Eagle Scout."

"That's why you're so good with fires?"

"That has nothing to do with it. I'm really just a pyromaniac like every other man on the planet."

"What is it with men and fire?"

"I think it's primordial, cavemen cooking their catch."

She smiled with understanding. "So, caveman. What's for dinner?"

I took two large foil packets from the cooler. "Patty melts with onions, carrots and potatoes."

I took the shovel and pushed away some of the coals. I filled two paper cups with water from the jug, then poured in each a packet of hot chocolate mix.

"How are we going to heat the water?" she asked.

"Watch this." Using a pair of tongs, I carefully set the paper cups in the flames.

She looked at me doubtfully. "*What* are you doing?"

"Just watch."

The flames ignited the wax rims of the cup, searing them both black, but nothing else burned. After a few minutes the chocolate was boiling in the paper cups. "That is so cool," Macy said. "How did you know it wouldn't melt the cup?"

"Life Scout," I said.

The sun set, leaving the campsite illuminated only by the fire and moonlight. I laid out silverware, and then I pulled our dinners from the fire. The foil was black with ashes and the juices sizzled inside. When I peeled back the foil, the food steamed in the cold air. I set one of the meals in front of Macy.

"Be careful, they're hot."

She poked at her dinner with a fork. "I can see that."

Macy speared a carrot, blew on it then ate it. She smiled. Then she tried the meat.

"That's really good. I've never cooked over a campfire before," Macy said, "or under it."

"I used to go camping with my friend and his dad. There's nothing better than food cooked over a campfire."

"Did your own dad ever take you camping?"

"There are two kinds of families in this world: those who camp and those who don't. We were a *don't*."

"The Hummels were a *don't* too. Dick— Mr. Hummel—took us once. It was also our last family outing."

"What happened?"

"Nothing in particular. It's just—some people make life harder than it needs to be. Everything in that home was a drama." She sighed. "I'm so glad I never have to see them again."

When we finished eating, I went back to my car and brought back two hangers I had unbent for roasting marshmallows. I reached into the sack and brought out a package of graham crackers, a bag of marshmallows and two Hershey chocolate bars. "S'mores," I said.

"I love s'mores."

"Of course you do. They're made with chocolate."

"You haven't known me for two weeks, and you already know all you need to know to get along with me."

Macy's marshmallows kept igniting like a torch until I taught her how to carefully rotate them above the coals. After we finished eating, I said, "I have one more surprise." I went back to my car and retrieved my guitar. She clapped when she saw it.

"I was hoping you'd play for me."

"I was hoping you'd say that."

We sat on the picnic bench facing the fire, and I played for nearly an hour. Being with Macy was wonderful. The moon was bright above us, illuminating the campground in a solemn blue hue beneath the trees' skeletal canopy. The snow dampened the sound of my guitar and the notes fell deep and stirring. Macy became very reflective and the flames from the fire danced in her eyes. After seven or eight songs I lay the guitar flat on the picnic table.

"I could listen to you for hours," Macy said softly.

"I love the guitar. There's no pretense to it. It is what it is."

"Sounds like you're talking about yourself," Macy said.

I didn't say anything.

"So why did you tell me to bring a swimsuit?"

I grinned. "Oh, that was just to throw you off the trail. You didn't bring it, did you?"

"I'm wearing it under my clothes."

"Sorry," I laughed.

She just shook her head. "So tell me something about Mark Smart that no one else in the whole world knows."

"Just about anything would fit that criteria."

"Then tell me something that no one would guess. Like, what's the weirdest thing you've ever done?"

I thought about it. "Okay. When I was seventeen, some buddies and I borrowed a mannequin from a thrift shop . . ."

She stopped me. "How do you *borrow* a mannequin?"

"Okay, we stole a mannequin. But we intended to return it."

"Go on."

"We borrowed a mannequin, then we carried it up the back of the drive-in movie theater, and then during the show we threw it off in front of the screen so it looked like someone jumped."

"That's pretty funny. Weird, maybe even a little twisted, but funny."

"Yeah, people were honking and stuff. We climbed down pretty fast and got out of there."

"With or without the mannequin?"

I had to think about it. "Without."

"So you really did steal it."

"Why are you so concerned about the mannequin?"

"I'm not. I just wanted to know if you're a thief."

"I *was* a mannequin thief. But now I'm reformed. I haven't stolen a single mannequin since then. In fact, I can walk through the entire menswear section at J. C. Penney's and never even touch one."

"Okay. *Reformed* mannequin thief. So what's your biggest dream?"

"Biggest dream would be to hear a song I wrote playing on the radio."

"That would be cool."

I nodded. "Yeah, it would be. But I would also be happy to just open up a little guitar shop somewhere and teach and sell guitars."

She smiled at this. "That sounds nice. Simple."

"Simple's good."

"Yeah, simple's good."

"So how about you? What's the weirdest thing you've ever done?"

Her mouth pursed a little. "Nothing I'd want to share."

"Hold on, I just shared with you my criminal activities . . ."

"Trust me on this."

I looked at her quizzically. I couldn't believe that she was capable of anything more criminal than tearing a DO NOT REMOVE label off a mattress.

"Okay, then what's your biggest dream?"

Her lips curved in a gentle smile. "My biggest dream is to have a family. Like the kind on TV reruns where there's a mother and a father and a couple kids and we eat dinner together at night and go on summer vacations to Yellowstone. I don't know if anyone does that anymore, but it's what I want."

I smiled at her fantasy. "Okay, so tell me a secret about you. It doesn't have to be criminal," I added.

She thought a moment. "Okay, there are two things. One *is* a little weird."

"Go on," I coaxed.

"I write poems."

"Poems?"

"I have a whole notebook of them."

"That's not weird."

"No, that's the other thing."

"Then we'll get to that later. Let's hear a poem."

"If I can remember one. I know, about a week ago I wrote a Christmas poem for Jo." Macy sat up straight as if delivering a formal recitation. "I should tell you that Jo just loves Christmas and she has all these traditions. One of them is we always read in Second Luke before we share gifts. My poem is called 'What Christmas Asks,' by Macy Wood." She cleared her throat. I smiled at her introduction.

"Our family gathers 'round open script,
A Yule observance yearly kept,
And reads the lines of Bible writ,
The story that all year has slept.
A Mother Mary in travail
In search of place that she might birth,
That sin and heartbreak not prevail,

A son to bring into the earth.
And as she crossed from door to door,
A stranger in unwelcome place,
Rejection met with each implore,
This small request from heaven's face.
And yet, we too must make this
    choice,
As Christmas moves from inn to inn,
If we will hear its gentle voice
And open up and let it in.
We read of shepherds who, in kind,
On darkened night watched o'er their
    sheep,
Then, beckoned once, left all behind
To find that holy child in sleep.
At Christmas we too are called,
To leave our troubled lives of care,
To set aside our burdened minds,
With God and man our hearts to
    share.
We read of wise men, traveled far,
Their gaze set on a bright new light
And lifted to exalted star,
Inspired by that celestial sight.
And Christmas too does ask of us,
To raise our eyes to higher spheres,
Believe the best in life and man,
Embrace new hope, release our fears.

And so this scripture, read anew,
Was not just penned for days all past.
With each new year our hearts renew
And this, of us, each Christmas asks."

She looked at me expectantly. "What do you think?"

I applauded. "Bravo. That was great."

"Thank you. Thank you very much," she replied theatrically. "Jo really liked it. She made me recite it, like, a dozen times."

"It's a good poem."

"Like I said, Jo's a real Christmasphile." The corners of her mouth rose. "I'm not sure that's a word."

"Sounds like one to me."

"You can tell by how our home was decorated. Jo gets the decorations out before Halloween."

"I saw them. How about you? You a fan of Christmas?"

She paused. "I'm warming to it. I had a long string of pretty bad Christmases."

"With your parents?"

"No, those were okay. At least what I can remember of them. But Christmas at the Hummels' isn't something I like to think about."

"What was it like—Scrooge?"

"No, actually, Irene bought a lot of gifts. Even for me. But gifts are easy. I just remember lining up with the other kids to say thank you and kiss her, and she would never let me. It was her way of reminding me I was different."

I frowned at this. "So what's the other thing you were thinking about telling me but thought was too weird?"

"I don't think I should tell you. You might think I'm . . . spooky. Or crazy."

"Spooky or crazy? Now you have to tell me."

"No, I don't."

"You can't set me up like that and then hold out."

"Of course I can. It's what girls do best."

I grinned. "Please."

"Okay. But don't think I'm weird. Promise me."

"I don't know what I'm promising, but I promise."

"Life Scout honor?"

"I'd go Eagle if I could."

"Okay then." She paused as if she were standing on the edge of a high dive unsure whether to jump or not. "Okay." She took a deep breath. "I have dreams that come true."

I nodded as if I knew what she meant. "What do you mean?"

"I dream about things and then they happen."

"What sort of things?"

"All sorts of things."

"Like what?"

"Well, for one, I dreamt you. The night before you came to the Hut, I had this dream that I was about to lock up the coffee shop when a snowman came to the door."

"A snowman?"

"You *were* covered in snow when I first saw you."

"Okay, it's a stretch, but I'll go with it. So what did this snowman want?"

"There's more. He wanted to use the phone because his sled was broken."

I raised one brow. "Okay, not bad."

"Then I gave him a ride home. So he wouldn't melt."

"Alright, that's eerie."

"I know. It happens a lot."

"How often?"

"Every few months. It usually happens before there's some big change, or be-

fore . . . before I meet someone who is going to be important in my life. I dreamt of Jo
just before I met her. At the time I was living
in a homeless shelter. I dreamt that this crying angel came and took me to her home."

"I think that's amazing."

"I don't know what to think of it. Not all
my dreams are special. Most of them are
just like everyone else's, but I can tell when
a dream is more than just a dream. It feels
different."

"In what way?"

"It's hard to explain. It feels more like a
memory. Sometimes I'll have the same
dream more than once."

"Have you had any more dreams about
me?"

"No. But I did have one last night that
bothered me."

"What was it?"

"I was looking for Noel, and for some reason I had to go back to the Hummels' to
find her. Noel was hiding in Mrs. Hummel's
bedroom, and I had to beg her to let her
out."

"Did she?"

"Yes. But I still didn't see her. I don't remember why."

"What do you think it means?"

She gestured with both hands. "That's the thing. I don't know. I never know. That's what I hate about it. What good is a dream when you can't understand it until after it comes true?" She shivered.

"It's getting really cold. Do you want to go back?"

"Not really. But maybe we could get closer. You know, to warm up?"

"I've just the thing." I took my guitar back to the car and brought back a thick wool blanket. I sat down next to her and threw the blanket over both of us.

"You had this all planned out," she said.

"Of course I did. This is the perfect place to bring a date. It's romantic, secluded and very cold."

"So this whole thing, the guitar, the blanket, the full moon, it was all just a setup?"

"I didn't have much to do with the moon, but besides that—yes."

She smiled. "Good."

We looked into each other's eyes, then simultaneously leaned forward and kissed for the first time. I don't remember the sequence of events after that, but it was all a pleasant blur. The softness and warmth of her body against mine, the happy sighs. The feeling of perfect contentment. An hour later our fire was dead and the temperatures had fallen well below freezing, too cold even for our body heat. So I started the car, and while Macy warmed up inside, I shoveled snow onto the fire pit. Then we drove back down to the valley. On the drive back I said, "Salt Lake has such great canyons. You and Joette must come up here all the time."

"No, we never come. Jo had something terrible happen up here."

"In Big Cottonwood Canyon?"

"Her little girl fell into the creek and drowned."

I turned and looked at her. "Where we just were?"

"No, it's a campsite a little ways up."

"How long ago was that?"

"About five years ago. Just before I met her."

"I'm sorry. I should have asked before I took you there."

"No, it's okay. I've been up there before. I just don't come up with Jo, and I won't tell her about us coming here tonight. It's not like she'd be mad or anything, it would just remind her." She turned to me. "So if she asks, tell her we went to Liberty Park."

"Liberty Park," I repeated. "*Will* she ask where we went?"

"Most definitely. You should know she's very protective of me. She'll be waiting up. That's just the way she is."

"That's nice," I decided.

"Yeah. It is." She turned to me. "I've been meaning to ask you—what are you doing for Thanksgiving?"

"Watching TV. Probably eating a TV dinner."

"That's pathetic. Come have dinner with us. It's going to be great this year. This is the first year in ten years Joette has the holiday off."

"People eat at Denny's on Thanksgiving Day?" I asked.

"Thanksgiving's a big day at Denny's. They have a turkey, mashed potatoes and dressing special with a piece of pumpkin pie for just $7.99. It's not bad."

I thought Macy sounded a little like an advertisement. In spite of her glowing review, I found the idea of eating Thanksgiving dinner there a little depressing. Of course someone who was planning on spending

Thanksgiving at home with a Hungry-Man turkey dinner shouldn't cast stones. Or, at least, cranberry sauce.

"Will Joette mind if I crash your dinner?" I asked.

"Of course not. She likes you."

"She doesn't know me."

"Better than you think. I tell her everything."

It was past midnight when I pulled in to Macy's driveway. The lights were still on inside the house. I killed the engine.

"Thank you for taking me out," she said. "It was fun."

"Thank you for going. It *was* fun. Especially the kissing part," I added.

She smiled. "That was fun." She looked into my eyes. "May I ask you something personal?"

"Sure."

"When we first met, you told me your girlfriend had just dropped you. Were you serious about her?"

"I don't know." I looked at Macy and smiled. "I guess that's the answer. If you don't know if you're serious, you're not. She wanted to get married."

"And you?"

"We talked about it. We'd dated forever, like four years. I just didn't know if she was the one. You'd think after four years you'd know."

"I think after four years you would have left if she wasn't. So what was she like?"

"Tennys was . . ." I hesitated. "Tennys is the kind of girl you describe in stereotypes."

"What do you mean?"

"She was popular. Homecoming queen, head cheerleader, you know."

Macy stifled a laugh.

"What?"

"It's just . . . I don't see you dating the homecoming queen."

I didn't tell her that I was voted homecoming king. "Why?"

"You're much . . . deeper."

"No, we're both pretty shallow. Between the two of us we couldn't make a decent wading pool."

Macy laughed. "What was her personality like? Typical snob?"

"No, Tennys was nice."

"Nice?"

"Yeah. She was really pleasant."

"What does that mean?"

"She just kind of went along with everything. No drama, no problems. The joy of the unexamined life."

"Just like me," Macy said, then burst out laughing. "You should have married her when you had the chance."

I smiled and pulled Macy closer. "Yeah, I probably should have."

"So are you still planning on coming to dinner tomorrow at Bonnie's?"

I had forgotten about it. "Of course. Do you want me to drive?"

"If you don't mind. I don't like driving that much."

"That's because you're bad at it."

She hit me. "I am not bad at it."

"Yes, you are. You almost hit a light post the night we met."

"It was a blizzard. I should have let you walk home like you were going to."

"You should have. Now you're stuck with me."

"Yeah. I hope so."

I leaned forward to kiss her again. The patio light began flashing on and off like a strobe light. Macy pulled back. "I told you."

"Is she serious?"

"No. She's just teasing. It's like an inside joke."

"This happens often?"

Macy smiled coyly. "Now and then."

"So what about you? Where's your boyfriend?"

"I've been on a hiatus from boys."

"For how long?"

"Since summer. Ever since I broke up with my last boyfriend."

"Were you serious?"

"Not as serious as he was." The lights began flashing again and she shook her head slowly. "She drives me crazy," she said happily. "I better go." She leaned forward and we kissed again, and again. Finally she whispered, "Good night."

"Good night."

She climbed out of the car and bounded up the walk. When she was inside, I started my car and drove home. I definitely could see myself getting too serious.

C H A P T E R

Seventeen

*Somewhere between the main course
and coffee, Mrs. Foster served up
a new paradigm.*

✦ MARK SMART'S DIARY ✦

We arrived at Bonnie's house a few minutes before one. We rang the bell and she hollered to us to let ourselves in. We found her in the kitchen, rushing from pot to pot. Macy stepped in to help. Bonnie assigned me to set the table, then take Fred, her dog, out for a "constitutional," which I did. All of us, dog included, finished our assignments about the same time. We gathered in the kitchen and sat down to eat.

Bonnie had cooked a pot roast along with fresh green beans, mashed potatoes and hot butter flake rolls. I hadn't eaten a meal like that since I left home. Halfway through the meal Bonnie asked, "How long have you been in Utah, Mark?"

My mouth was full, and I had to finish chewing and swallow before I could answer . . . "I came here about a year and a half ago."

"How often do you go back home?"

"I haven't been back since I came."

"I bet your parents miss you."

"Mark just lost his mother," Macy said.

She looked at me sympathetically. "I'm sorry. That's a hard thing. How's your father holding up?"

"I think he's okay."

"I'm sure he misses you. Especially at a time like this." She turned to Macy. "Would you pass the beans, dear?"

"Sure."

Bonnie took the bowl, and as she spooned green beans onto her plate, she said casually to Macy, "Speaking of fathers, I found yours."

Both of our heads swiveled toward her. "You found him?" Macy asked.

"I was going to call you last night but it was so late. It was past nine."

Considering that neither of us got off work before eleven, I found this amusing.

"How did you find him?" Macy asked.

"I remembered that about six months after you were taken away, your father remarried. It didn't last long; I don't think it was more than a few months. But I found the invitation." She turned to me. "I never throw those things out. The woman he married still lives in Kearns. I hope you don't mind, but I took the liberty of calling her. She said he's been living at a friend's house. That's probably why you couldn't find him listed anywhere."

"Did she give you his address?" Macy asked.

"No. Just her own. She says she wants to meet you. Anyway I wrote her address down. It's on the fridge. I'll get it."

She pushed back from the table and went to the kitchen. She returned a moment later holding a sticky note.

"Her name is Barbara Norris, and she lives at 500 Altura Road in Kearns. She said that's about 616 West. She's in Apartment 321."

She handed the paper to Macy.

"Bonnie, thank you."

"You'll have to let me know how everything turns out. Now let's get on with our dinner before everything gets cold."

CHAPTER

Eighteen

Our journey feels like a board game where each throw of the dice lands us on some new square. What a peculiar square we landed on today.

✦ MARK SMART'S DIARY ✦

I noticed that Macy hadn't eaten much since Bonnie's announcement. I'm sure it was all she could do to not jump up from the table and race over to the woman's house. Over Bonnie's objections we did the dishes, then went into the living room for dessert and coffee. Bonnie took out some music rolls and fired up the player piano. When I saw that Bonnie would probably keep us all night, I apologetically told her that I had to get home. Macy knew I had no place to be and she looked at me gratefully. Macy promised to return next Sunday and we said goodbye. When we got in the car, Macy turned to me and said, "Thank you." Then she handed me the paper with the woman's address.

In ten minutes we were standing at the doorstep of the third-story apartment. Macy pressed the doorbell. Then she looked down at the welcome mat, shifting nervously from foot to foot. We heard ap-

proaching steps, and the door opened until the chain caught, revealing half of a
woman's face. "Yes?"

"We're looking for Barbara Norris," I said.

"I'm Barbara Norris."

"I'm Macy Wood," Macy said.

It took a moment for the name to register.
"Ah." She shut the door to unlatch the
chain then swung the door open. "My gosh,
I didn't expect you to be so old." She
glanced at me. "And this is?"

"This is my friend, Mark."

"Hi," I said.

She waved dramatically. "Come in. Come
in, both of you."

Macy walked in first and Barbara
wrapped her arms around her. "Welcome
back, honey. Welcome, welcome, welcome." Macy just kind of absorbed the
greeting. I shut the door and stood a few
feet back, watching. When she had released Macy, she went for me. "I don't know
you, but if you're with our baby, you're family."

The woman left me breathless. "Yes,
ma'am."

"Now sit, both of you. Not there, over on
the couch." She pushed me toward the

ugliest piece of furniture I'd ever seen—a gaudy green, red and gold patterned sofa-sleeper. She sat down on the only other piece of furniture in the room—a wooden chair from the kitchen dinette set. For a moment she just looked at Macy. "You know, your father talks about you all the time. He carries a picture of you in his wallet. But you were just a child. My gosh."

"No, I didn't know that," Macy said.

"Of course you didn't. And here you are. I've wanted to meet you since the first time your daddy told me about you." She looked at me. "Do miracles ever cease?"

"I don't know," I said. I wasn't sure if she expected an answer but she looked like she did.

"They don't, believe me, they don't."

"You were married to my father?" Macy asked.

"If you can call it that. I've had colds that lasted longer." She looked at Macy and her voice dropped an octave. "I don't know how much you know about your father. But he's a drug addict."

"Yes, I know," Macy said. "Did you?"

"Not at first. But by the time I found out, I was already in love with the man." She looked at me and rolled her eyes. "You know, love conquers all." She laughed dramatically. "Yeah, right. He was just another in a long line of fixer-uppers."

"Mrs. Foster said that you know where my father is," Macy said.

"Yes, we still talk all the time. We're much better friends now that we're divorced."

"Does he live far from here?"

"I don't think your dad's ever ventured far from here. You know your dad."

Macy just frowned. "No. I really don't."

"Right. I'll stop saying that. I'm sure you're just poppin' to see him. I just want you to be prepared. He's pretty sick."

"From the drugs?"

"And everything else he's abused his body with. God knows what's keeping him alive. He needs a liver transplant, but he's so high-risk that the doctors denied him. I think the hospital sent him home to die. He's been living over at a buddy's place." She looked into Macy's eyes. "He is very excited about seeing you."

"He knows I'm looking for him?"

"I told him last night after that woman called. He asked me to put you on the line the minute you arrived." She bent over and lifted a portable phone from the floor next to her chair. "Are you ready?"

Macy glanced at me and took a deep breath. "Yes."

Barbara dialed the number from memory, then handed the receiver to Macy. Macy held it up to her ear as Barbara and I watched.

"Hello. Is Marshall Wood there?"

There was a pause.

"Daddy? This is Macy."

C H A P T E R

Nineteen

We found Macy's father.
I learned something valuable today.
Oftentimes the greatest hurts of
our lives come from running
from the smaller ones.

✦ MARK SMART'S DIARY ✦

Macy's father lived less than three miles from his ex-wife's home, on the south end of the Kearns city line. The area wasn't exactly the high-rent district, and the homes were all cracker boxes neatly built along narrow streets lined with older cars.

As I pulled in to the crumbling cement driveway, my car bottomed out loudly on the gutter, alerting the home's residents of our arrival. I noticed someone brush back the front curtains and then disappear.

I shut off the car and then looked over at Macy. This was the third time I'd sat with her anticipating a meeting that could change her life. Only this time we knew whom we'd find. Macy looked very tense, and she was fidgeting with a ring on her finger. "What are you thinking?" I asked.

"A million different things. It's weird, I've anticipated this moment my entire life, but I still don't know how I'm supposed to act.

What if I lose it? What if I totally freak out and scream at him for what he did to us?"

"Then he deserves it." I reached over and took her hand. "Just do what comes naturally. Whatever that is, it will be the right thing."

She looked at me soulfully, and I realized how vulnerable and afraid she was. I couldn't help but think how beautiful her eyes were. "Thank you for being here," she said.

I looked at her and grinned. "How did I get in the middle of all this?"

"You asked to use my phone."

"I really need to get me one of those portable phones," I said.

"You need to get a phone—period," she said.

"That Barbara woman was . . . interesting."

Macy suddenly grinned. "Interesting as in fascinating or interesting as in a nightmare?"

I smiled back. "Yes."

"Maybe my father's the same way."

"That would explain a lot about you."

"You're so mean," she laughed, and it

was good to see her relax. She squeezed
my hand. "All right, let's go."

We climbed out of the car and walked
up to the door. The front porch was sup-
ported by two painted wood beams, both
chipped and scarred. A wind chime made
from flattened tin forks and spoons hung
from the portico. There was no doorbell,
so I knocked. Almost immediately a man
opened the door. He was bald and short,
maybe in his late fifties, and with a belly
that hung over the waist of his pants. He
glanced over me, then his eyes settled on
Macy. She looked at him, unsure if this was
her father or not.

I sensed her confusion. "Mr. Wood?" I
asked.

"No, I'm Ken. Marshall's in bed." He
turned to Macy. "Your dad's waiting for
you."

I put my hand on her back. "Go ahead."

She stepped inside, and we followed Ken
to a bedroom at the end of the hallway.
Macy stepped into the open doorway and
stopped. Then she raised both hands together, cupping them over her mouth. I
stepped up behind her and looked over her
shoulder. Her father lay in bed propped up

by pillows, the sheets pulled up to his waist. I'd never seen a grown man that thin. He had an oxygen tube curled around his ears to his nostrils. His eyes were sunken and full of tears.

"Baby!" he called.

Macy couldn't talk.

"Come here, baby."

She went to him and she fell forward into his embrace. They were both weeping.

"Finally home," he said, crushing her hair with his fingers. "Finally home." Ken and I stepped into the room and watched the reunion.

"I've missed you," he said.

"I've missed you too," Macy said.

"Look, Ken. Look how beautiful my little girl is."

"I can see."

He looked at me. "This your boyfriend?"

Without looking, Macy said, "Yes."

"I'm Mark," I said.

"Nice to know you," he said.

"Nice to know you, sir."

He said to Macy, "How long has it been?"

"Fourteen years, one month, two weeks, three days."

He shook his head. "Do you remember our last day together?"

"We did all the seasons."

"That's right. I thought I might not ever see you again. So I wanted to get in all the memories I could. Easter. Halloween. Christmas. Do you still have that ornament from your mother?"

"Yes. I've carried it every place I've gone."

"Those ornaments were so important to your mother. She even spoke of them as she was dying. Your sister Noel has one just like it."

Macy reacted to hearing Noel's name, almost as if it was delivered with a low-voltage shock. She moved back from him. "Tell me about Noel. Do you still see her?"

He was quiet for a moment, then he burst out in a fit of coughing. "No. I haven't seen her since they took her from me." He saw the disappointment in Macy's face. "That's what I regret most of all—apart from losing the both of you—was separating the two of you. It never should have happened. I promised your mother that I wouldn't let it happen." He suddenly choked up. "But I did."

Macy rubbed his arm. "I remember so little about her. It's like she's there, in my head somewhere, but just out of reach." She looked at him somberly. "Tell me about her."

"Do you remember what your ornament said on it?"

"Noel. December 25."

"That was Noel's first Christmas. She was born Christmas Day. I wanted to name her Holly. But with the last name of Wood, your mama wouldn't go for that. So we named her Christina Noel. Your mama wanted Christine for the Christ child."

"I couldn't remember her name . . ." Macy confessed.

"Losing her was traumatic for you, baby. You probably don't remember, but you were her mother. You'd fix her breakfast, dress her, bathe her. A counselor at the rehab told me that when parents aren't there, the oldest kid often takes over. He said they found out about me because every day you brought potato chip sandwiches to school." He exhaled loudly. "I wasn't much good before your mother died. But after . . ." He looked at her sadly.

"I was only five when mom died."

He nodded, ashamed. "Yeah, you were."

"Do you know *where* Noel is?"

"No. They first took her to a foster home,

then another family adopted her. I had to sign away my rights. I was in rehab then, and now my head's full of sawdust. I don't remember things too well. But I'm sure someone at the state knows."

Macy frowned. "The state won't tell me. Her file was sealed."

For a moment the energy drained from the room. Then her father's face lit up. "I know someone who'd know."

"Who?" Macy asked eagerly

"That woman who adopted you. Hummel."

Macy's face flashed with pain. "Why would *she* know?"

"The caseworker told me that the family that took Noel had problems. She cried for you for weeks. Finally the family tried to find you. Don't you remember?"

"I saw her once. It was at our adoption hearing. I remember Mrs. Hummel getting into a fight with the woman who was with Noel. Then I never saw her again."

He frowned. "That's a shame." There was silence. "How long have you been looking for me?" her father asked.

"Not too long. But I've thought about seeing you my whole life—wondering what would happen if I were to bump into you at a gas station or at the supermarket."

He nodded at this. "I was hoping you'd come."

"Why didn't you come to find me?"

"I was afraid. I was sure you'd hate me."

Macy didn't answer immediately. "I don't hate you."

"You should hate me, sister. I let you down. I let the whole family down."

"You couldn't help it . . ."

"Macy, don't make excuses for me. There's no excuse for what I did. Was there ever a good enough excuse for a father to abandon his children?"

"I don't know," Macy said.

For a moment they both just stared into each other's eyes. "You should know there's a reason. Not an excuse, but a reason. I know it don't hardly matter now, you can't change the past, but I never set out to be the failure I am. When I was seven, I got polio. They gave me pain medications by the bucketful. I never stopped using them. I couldn't stop. Looking back . . ." He shook his head. "If I'd known what it would cost me, I would've chosen the pain. The greatest hurts of our lives come from running from the smaller hurts."

Macy stepped back and for a moment she just looked at him. I couldn't tell what she was thinking, but I saw something in her I had never seen before—someone much older than the young woman I had met just a few weeks earlier. She touched the corner of her eye, then said softly, "I've suffered, Dad. Far more than anyone knows. I was sexually abused in the drug treatment center they sent you to. I was beaten almost every week by the evil woman who adopted me. I lived on the street for three months. For six weeks I slept behind a dumpster at a Wal-Mart. You'd be surprised what you'd do for a cheese sandwich when you haven't eaten in four days. You're right. I should hate you. But I don't. I pity you. No matter what I've been through, I've never given away anything I should have kept. And I've never betrayed anyone I've ever loved. Nothing could be worse than that."

He began to sob. "I'm so sorry, baby. I'm so sorry."

Macy's voice softened. "I need to go now," she said. Macy leaned forward and held him.

When he could speak, he asked, "Will I see you again?"

She nodded. "We've got a lot to catch up on."

He continued to weep as Macy walked out of the room. I glanced back once more at him before I left. I pitied him too.

Macy was quiet for most of the drive home. I couldn't imagine what she was thinking. When we stopped at an intersection on State Street, she erupted, "Why do I have to go back there? Why does *that* woman have to be part of this?"

I glanced over at her. "Remember, you dreamed about this; that you had to go back to the Hummels' to find Noel."

"It's not fair."

"Maybe there's a reason you need to go back."

"Yeah," she said sarcastically, "like I haven't suffered enough."

"Maybe it's because you have."

She didn't answer me, just looked out the window the rest of the way home. It was late and I sensed that she wanted to be alone, so I dropped her off, then went back to my apartment.

CHAPTER
Twenty

I don't know exactly how or when it happened, but Macy has me.

✦ MARK SMART'S DIARY ✦

Once, in a church sermon, I heard a preacher say that if you drop a frog into a pan of boiling water, it will hop out. But if you drop the frog into cool water then add boiling water a teaspoon at a time, you can boil it alive.

The preacher was speaking metaphorically about sin—which is good because I don't know why anyone would want to boil a frog. But I think the preacher could have used the same analogy about romantic love as well. Sometimes love happens so gradually that by the time you realize you're in it, you're already cooked—if you'll pardon the pun. At least that's the way it was with Macy and me.

I couldn't tell you when I decided to ask Macy to marry me, but it was on the way home from her father's house that I first realized that I had.

To an onlooker, I know this probably seems crazy. After all, I'd only known Macy for three weeks, but it *seemed* much longer. To misquote Frost, what my feelings lacked in length they made up for in height. I was madly, head-over-heels, pinch-me-if-I'm-dreaming in love with this girl. I wanted us to be together and couldn't imagine any other alternative. When you've finally met the one person you want to spend the rest of your life with, you want the rest of your life to start as soon as possible. I decided Thanksgiving was the right time to pop the question.

CHAPTER
Twenty-one

Today Macy confronted her greatest fear and in doing so, herself. Usually life's greatest gifts come wrapped in adversity.

✦ MARK SMART'S DIARY ✦

The school was closed Monday for parent-teacher conferences, and I had to go in to work early. I was finished by three and called Macy on the way home to check up on her. "I'm going to see Irene," she told me. Her voice sounded hard with determination.

"Do you want me to go with you?"

"I have to do this alone. Will you come over later tonight?"

"Yes. What time?"

"About eight."

"I'll be there. Good luck."

"Thanks. I'll need it."

.✦.

Driving back to the old neighborhood filled Macy with dread. The Hummel home was only five miles from where she and Joette currently lived, but in Macy's mind it had been relegated to another part of the world.

Or solar system. Her hands were clammy with cold sweat and she wiped them on her pant legs.

The street was shorter and narrower than she remembered. It had been almost seven years since she'd been there, and she felt like a war veteran returning to the scene of a great battle. It looked so harmless and peaceful now.

She parked across the street from the house. It hadn't changed much since she left, though it too looked smaller than she remembered. Very little ever changed at the Hummel house by design; only by neglect and deterioration.

There was an old tomato-red Dodge truck parked in the driveway with a yellow snow-plow mounted on its front and a magnetic sign on the driver's side door that read HUMMEL YARD CARE.

Macy stepped out of her car, walked up to the front door and knocked firmly, as if to prove to herself the strength of her resolve. She didn't bother with the doorbell. It had never worked while she lived there, and she knew no one would ever get around to fixing it.

Bart answered the door. Macy hadn't

seen him since she left. Even when they were children he was much bigger than she, and he'd grown considerably: he was now nearly a foot taller than Macy. Even though it was winter, he wore basketball shorts and a T-shirt. His jaw was shaded with stubble and he held a can of cheap beer in one hand. He looked at her and a smile of recognition crossed his face. "Hey, Mace!"

"Hi, Bart."

"What are you doing here? Come in."

She was surprised by his welcome. She stepped inside the house. The house looked almost the same as when she left—in fact, it looked the same as when she first came to the Hummels'. The one change was a new armoire with a television inside.

As she looked around the room, memory and resentment poured in like water into a capsizing boat. The house still stunk of dog and it made her nauseous. She wondered how she'd lived with it for all those years. She expected Buster to come charging in at any moment growling and threatening as he did with all intruders. He didn't.

"Buster still around?"

"Nah. He died a couple years back." Bart shut the door behind her. "Want a beer?"

"No thanks."

He pointed to the sofa. "Take a load off."

Macy looked around cautiously. There was no sign of Irene. She sat down on the sofa. The fabric on the cushions was worn thin, and the springs gave more than they should for a person her size.

"I didn't think we'd ever see you again."

Macy looked at the cold piece of buttered toast sitting on the cushion next to her and wondered how old it was. She set it on the armrest. "Neither did I."

Bart sat down across from her, holding the can with both hands between his legs.

"You got really pretty. You married?"

"No."

"So what brings you around?"

"I came to see Irene. Is she here?"

"She's always here."

"She doesn't leave anymore?"

"The house?" he asked, as if she were joking. "Nah, she leaves the bedroom sometimes, but not even that much anymore." He lifted the can to his mouth and drained it. "She mostly just lays in there and hollers for me."

"Is she sleeping now?"

"That or watching TV." He crushed the

can in his hand. "So where do you live? Are you still in Utah?"

"I live downtown."

He nodded. "How's your place?"

"It's nice. I have a roommate." Macy glanced nervously toward the hall, wondering if Irene might choose this time to make a rare appearance.

"So what do you need to talk to her about?"

"I'm looking for my sister."

Bart looked at her quizzically. "Sheryl's in Colorado."

"My *real* sister."

Just then a shrill screech came from the hallway. "Bart!" A sardonic smile crossed Bart's face as if to say *See what I put up with?* Not thirty seconds later it came again with the same intensity. "Bart!"

"What!" he shouted back.

"Who's there?"

He looked at Macy. "She's really on one today. It's one of her migraine days. You sure you want to see her?"

"I'm sure I *don't* want to. But I need to."

"Okay." He stood. "C'mon."

They walked to the door at the end of the darkened hallway. Bart opened the door slightly, stepping into the shadow of the room. The light was off and the blinds were drawn. Macy slipped in behind him.

"Who's here?" Irene asked. Her voice was low and grating. All Macy could make out was a large mass in the bed. The top of the mass turned. "Who's that with you?"

"It's Macy."

"Who?"

"Macy. Your daughter."

The mass didn't move. "What does it want?"

"Why don't you ask her?"

Macy moved closer to the bed. She could now make out the woman underneath the blankets. Irene had gained at least fifty pounds, and Macy was surprised to see how much she had aged in the years since she left. Macy spoke calmly. "I came to see if you know where my sister Noel is."

The woman reached over and took a drink from a glass on the nightstand. She choked on it. After she stopped gagging, she said, "Why would I know that?"

"Because you know who her adopted parents are."

Irene sniffed a little. "I don't know what you're talking about."

"Yes, you do. I need to know what their last name is."

Irene again reached for her glass and took another drink, followed by an even greater eruption of coughing. She wiped her mouth with her arm. "Where you been?"

"I need to know what Noel's parents' name is."

"Can't help you," she said, turning over.

Macy exhaled in frustration. Bart approached the bed. "Tell her, mother."

"I won't," she said, sounding absurdly childish.

"Tell her now."

Mrs. Hummel said nothing.

"Okay. I'm calling." He walked to the phone and lifted the receiver. "I should have done this months ago." He pressed several numbers on the keypad.

"Wait, don't," Irene said. There was panic in her voice.

"Then tell her."

The woman's anxiety was palpable.

"Better hurry, it's ringing."

"It's Thorup," she bleated.

"Thorup?" Bart echoed.

"He's a lawyer. Lived up in one of them fancy rich neighborhoods on the mountain."

Bart hung up the phone.

"Are you sure?" Macy asked.

"Course I'm sure," she said bitterly. "You don't forget a name like Thorup. Sounds like 'throw up.' "

Macy just shook her head, then looked over at Bart. "Thank you." She walked to the door.

"Where you going?!" Irene shouted.

"Home," Macy said.

Bart followed her out to the front porch. Macy stopped to talk to him. "Thanks for your help."

"Least I could do. You okay?"

"Yeah." She cocked her head. "Who were you calling?"

"Actually no one. But she thought I was calling the old folks home. It's like a cattle prod. I just keep threatening to have her sent away. Sometimes it's the only way to get her to do something." He frowned. "It had to be hard for you . . . coming back here."

"I thought it would be worse. You know, you build some people up in your mind, and they become powerful and frightening. When I saw her lying there, all I felt was pity."

"I'm sorry about how she treated you. How we all treated you."

Macy looked at him thoughtfully. "You've grown up."

Bart smiled but didn't reply.

"Where's Ronny and Sheryl?"

"Ron got married and joined the army. He's stationed in Maryland. Sheryl got married too, but she's already divorced. She lives in Boulder with her little boy."

"What about you? What are you up to?"

"I mow my lawns. In the winter I push snow. And between that I take care of Mom."

"Lucky you."

"Someone's gotta do it. But it's not all bad. She keeps to her room most the time. It's free rent and she's got cable." He rubbed his nose. "I don't think she'll be around much longer. Doctor says she has early-onset old-timers; half the time she don't know where she is. You're lucky you asked her before she forgot."

"I guess I am." Macy leaned forward and for the first time in her life, she and her brother hugged. "Take care, Bart."

"You too."

Macy stepped down the sidewalk. When she got to the curb, Bart shouted after her.

"Hey."

She turned.

"Don't be a stranger. Come 'round sometime."

Macy managed a half smile. "You take care of yourself." She walked to her car, and for the first time she truly left the Hummels behind.

C H A P T E R
Twenty-two

Tonight Macy fell asleep in my arms. I'm not sure that Heaven could be anything more than that.

✦ MARK SMART'S DIARY ✦

I was waiting for Macy when she got home. We sat together on the couch, the room dark except for the dancing indigo glow of the television. We weren't as interested in the show as we were in holding each other. At the end of the program I shut off the television, leaving the room completely dark and momentarily silent. Macy snuggled into me.

"Mark, I'm scared," she said softly.

"Of what?"

"Of finding her." More silence. "You know, I feel like I've come all this way to stop a foot in front of the finish line. I don't know if I can do this."

Just then the grandmother's clock in the entryway struck one, followed by a Winchester chime. When the sound dissipated, I said. "Are you afraid that she won't care?"

She took a deep breath. "What if she doesn't?"

"I don't know." I ran my fingers back

through her hair. "But do you know what would be worse?"

"What?"

"If she had been waiting for you her whole life and you never went because you were afraid."

She was quiet a long time. "You're pretty smart sometimes."

"Only sometimes?"

"Just sometimes."

I pulled her in closer, then lightly tickled her back with my hand. When Joette came home, Macy was asleep on my chest.

CHAPTER

Twenty-three

I have never felt truly at ease around the clean, shiny people of this world. Life has taught me the most trustworthy and honest are usually those who are frayed around the edges. Not always but usually.

✦ MARK SMART'S DIARY ✦

It wasn't hard for Macy to find the Thorups' address. There were only two Thorups in the Salt Lake Valley and only one on the East Side. Still, it was two more days, the day before Thanksgiving, before Macy was ready to see Noel.

The Thorups lived in a well-groomed development of upper-middle-class homes—a demographic of soccer moms and luxury automobiles. Macy had never driven to this part of Salt Lake before. The snow on the ground was substantially deeper than in the valley, and the plows had left snowbanks in front of the homes more than a yard high in some places.

The Thorup home was at the end of a cul-de-sac lined with tall winter-barren trees that overhung the street. Macy rechecked the address, then parked her car in front of the house. She climbed out of her car and stared at the home in awe.

Noel lived in a two-story French chateau

with a stone and glazed-stucco façade. Near the front door was a turret that rose nearly thirty feet and was capped with a weathered verdigris-copper roof and finial. The garage alone was bigger than Macy's home, she thought, and it made her happy to think her sister had grown up in such a palace. It was the most beautiful house she'd ever seen.

The yard was edged with flat-trimmed shrubs. There were plastic reindeer on the front lawn and even though it was daytime, the Christmas lights had been left on. A Volvo station wagon with the dealer's paper license plate still in the back window sat in the cobblestone driveway.

Macy walked slowly up the brick-lined walkway to the entrance, an enormous portico that protruded from the turret. The front door was a massive slab of oak, arched on top, with raised paneling engraved with hand-sized fleurs-de-lis. The center of the door was adorned with a large Christmas wreath of grapevine, holly and eucalyptus tied with ribbon and ornamented with pomegranates.

In front of the door was a seasonal red-and-green doormat that read WELCOME

SANTA, which was partially eclipsed by a flyer announcing the local Boy Scout troop's annual Thanksgiving food drive. Noel's home was more than across town. It was a whole different world.

Macy stood on the doorstep for a moment, her breath clouding in the air in front of her. Thoughts began flooding into her head and the reality of the impending meeting filled her with panic. Would she recognize her sister when she saw her? Would her sister know her? What would she say if she didn't? *Hi, you don't know me, but I'm your sister.*

There was a massive brass doorknocker in the center of the wreath; Macy knocked with it three times. Though she thought she heard movement inside the house, no one came to the door. She pressed the doorbell. There was a bright, lengthy chime inside the home, followed by soft, quick footsteps.

The door was opened by an attractive woman who looked to be in her late forties. She was thin, with short, blond hair. She wore a gray wool turtleneck with a silver, flat-linked chain with three pearls, pearl earnings, a gray wool skirt and black leather pumps. Though she smiled at Macy, there was cautiousness behind her cheerful façade. "May I help you?"

Macy dug her hands deeper in her pockets. "Hi. Mrs. Thorup? I'm looking for Noel."

The woman looked at her quizzically. "Noel?"

"Christina Noel?"

The woman's expression became even more strained. "No one's called her that for a long time. Christy isn't here."

Christy? "Do you expect her back soon? I can wait."

"Christy's not living here. May I ask who you are?"

Something about the way the woman asked made Macy even more uncomfortable. Then the woman's expression showed sudden understanding. "You're Macy, aren't you?"

"Yes, ma'am."

"Of course you are. You look like Christy." The woman stepped back, unblocking the entry. "I was just on my way out, but you can come in for a minute."

Macy looked around, suddenly apprehensive about entering the house.

"Come in. Let's talk."

"Thank you." Macy stepped inside the

marble-floored foyer. Above her a Strauss crystal chandelier hung from the center of the turret surrounded by a spiraled staircase that climbed to a second-story landing.

Mrs. Thorup led her into the front parlor, a spacious room with beautiful amber carpet, vaulted ceilings and alabaster sconces on the walls. On one end of the room, near the fireplace, was a horseshoe-shaped Steinway grand piano. In the center of the room a perfect blue spruce Christmas tree reached nearly to the top of the ceiling and filled the room with its aroma. The tree was professionally decorated with ornaments and ribbon that looked as luxurious as the home itself.

There were several still-life oil paintings on the walls, but the piece that drew Macy's attention was a large gold-framed family portrait. She guessed that the photograph had been taken many years earlier; the woman was a younger version of the one who had answered the door. A tall smiling man and three children stood behind her. The two teenaged boys were blond and blue-eyed; the young girl was auburn-haired and didn't look a thing like the rest of the family. She looked like Macy.

Mrs. Thorup sat down in a wingback chair and crossed her legs. She motioned to the couch across from her. "Sit down. Please."

Macy turned from the picture and sat on the crushed-velvet sofa across from the woman. Macy folded her hands in her lap. Christmas carols played softly in the background. Macy realized that she'd seen this woman before—a long, long time ago at the adoption hearing.

"My husband and I wondered if you might show up some day. Though I'm a little surprised you were able to find us."

"It wasn't easy," Macy said lightly, hoping for some sign of friendliness. The woman's face remained somber, if not grim. Macy swallowed nervously. "Did you say Noel doesn't live here anymore?"

"My daughter's away at college."

"Oh. Where does she go to school?"

Mrs. Thorup looked uncomfortable. After a moment she said, "The thing is, Christy doesn't know that you exist. In fact, she doesn't even know that she was adopted."

Macy looked at her in astonishment. "What? How could she not know?"

"She was only four . . ." Mrs. Thorup said.

"But we were so close. And the adoption

at the courthouse . . . How could she have forgotten that?"

Mrs. Thorup nodded. "The mind does what it needs to to survive."

Macy was exasperated. "You never told her about me?"

Mrs. Thorup squirmed a little in her chair. "Chuck and I felt the circumstances of Christy's early life were, as you said, traumatic enough. So we requested that all ties be severed, and the judge ordered her file sealed. *Especially* after the disastrous encounter with your family at the courthouse. So your coming here . . ." She was obviously pained. "We feel it's best that she doesn't know about you."

"And why would that be for the best?"

Mrs. Thorup seemed disturbed that Macy still didn't understand. "What could she possibly gain by knowing she was abandoned by her biological parents?"

"Well, for one, she would gain me."

"Is that a good thing?"

Macy was beginning to dislike this woman. "Yes. It is."

"You need to understand that in my daughter's mind, she doesn't have a sister.

She has two older brothers and us. How do you think seeing you would affect her?"

Macy had wondered the same thing. "I don't know."

"That's right, we don't know. Do you think it's fair to experiment with her life?"

What about any of this is fair? Macy thought, but didn't voice the question. "How is she?"

"She's wonderful. And she's smart as a whip. She was her high school salutatorian. She was awarded a full-ride scholarship to A.S.—" She caught herself. "To college." She glanced at the grand piano. "You should hear her play the piano. She's won several competitions."

"I'd like to," Macy said, even though she knew Mrs. Thorup hadn't meant it literally. She looked back at the woman. "Don't you think she'd want to know she has a sister?"

Mrs. Thorup repositioned herself in her chair. "You have to consider *her* reality." She suddenly smiled. Macy didn't trust it. "You seem like a nice young lady. You need to ask yourself, is this about her or you? Given what I remember about your own family situation, I'm sure you haven't had an easy time, and I understand why you want to . . .

reconnect with your sister. But if you really care about Christy, you should do the right thing. She has a wonderful life and a loving family. She's happy. Bringing something like this into her life is . . . well, it's a problem, isn't it?"

Macy couldn't believe the final turn her journey had taken.

"I'm sorry, honey. But I care about my daughter. I'm sure you want to do the right thing too."

Macy felt herself growing angry at the woman's condescending manner, but a part of her feared the woman might be right. They were clearly at an impasse, and in any case, there was nothing she could do now. Macy stood. "You must be busy. I'll let you go."

"Yes, I have an appointment." The woman quickly rose to her feet, obviously relieved to be done with the meeting. Then Macy noticed an ornament on the Christmas tree. She walked over to it and crouched down. It was bright red and written on its face in gold glitter was the word NOEL; it was a twin to the one she had been given by her father. Macy stood back up. "Do you have a pen and paper?"

The woman looked at her thoughtfully. "I'll get them for you."

She walked out of the room and returned carrying a pad and a plastic ballpoint pen with the name of her husband's law firm printed across it. She handed them both to Macy.

"Thank you." Macy wrote down her phone number and address. "This is where I live. In case you change your mind."

The woman took the note and Macy guessed what she was thinking—*In that case it doesn't matter.* "You can keep the pen," Mrs. Thorup said. She led Macy to the front door and opened it for her. A gust of cold air filled the foyer.

"It's been nice meeting you," the woman said unconvincingly then, a little more sympathetically, "Good luck."

"Thank you." Macy was about to leave without saying anything more but to her own surprise stopped and turned back, looking the woman in the eyes. "You know, you can call her Christy or whatever else you want, but changing her name doesn't change who she is or where she's from, or, as you say, 'her reality.' It's Noel's life, not yours. Good or bad, every minute of it belongs to her. You're a pretty lady. You have a lovely home. Everything's all perfect and clean. You probably never hit your children. I'm sure Noel's lucky to have you as a mother. But it still doesn't make it your life, and what she does with it shouldn't be your decision."

The woman swallowed, clutching the paper in her hand. Macy stepped out into the cold. "Goodbye."

"Goodbye," Mrs. Thorup said.

Macy walked back to her car, the tears now falling freely down her cheeks. The woman shut the door. She glanced back down at the paper in her hand then crumpled it up, walked into the kitchen and threw it away. Then she called her husband at the law office. "Chuck, you'll never believe who just came to the house."

C H A P T E R
Twenty-four

My disappointment tonight is only matched in depth by the hope the morning held.

✦ MARK SMART'S DIARY ✦

THANKSGIVING

Back home in Alabama, Thanksgiving was more an event than a meal. My mother and my Aunt Marge would start the preparations weeks in advance. First they would plan the menu (a ritual I never fully understood, as they always settled on the same dishes), then they would comb the paper, hunting for coupons and sales with no less intensity than our ancestors might have hunted a turkey or deer for the feast. Then they would compile their lists and begin the shopping, returning from each trip with a car full of grocery bags.

Thanksgiving dinner was always delight-fully gluttonous: the centerpiece of the meal, the turkey, could have graced the cover of a women's magazine, its skin brown and translucent as wax paper, the meat running with juices. There were chitterlings smoth-ered in tomato gravy and hot sauce, deviled eggs sprinkled with paprika, giblet dressing, collard greens with ham hocks spiced with dill pickle juice, turnip greens, fried okra, squash casserole, and corn bread dressing, with pitchers of sweet iced tea to drown it all down.

Then there were the essential desserts: pecan and sweet potato pies, and if the women felt especially ambitious, banana-bread pudding generously drizzled with sweetened condensed milk.

Before each meal Stu gave thanks to the Lord and prayed for the less fortunate, who, in light of such culinary excess, pretty much included everyone not dining with us.

The two families, my mom and Aunt Marge and my four cousins, always shared the meal. We dressed up in our Sunday-go-to-meeting best, which, after dinner, became our football uniforms. Mom always used her china, and the silverware made its annual outing from its wood felt-lined cabinet. We children would hand-polish each piece before laying it down on the white embroidered tablecloth.

This was all a stark contrast to the Thanksgiving I had planned to spend this year with a Hungry-Man TV dinner with turkey, dressing and spiced apples. I was grateful that Macy had invited me to share Thanksgiving with her and Joette. Still, I felt a bit melancholy as I thought of those Thanksgivings at home with my mother, homesick for a memory I could never return to.

I spent the morning watching football on television. Around noon I showered and dressed up in my best: an oxford shirt, sweater and slacks. Then I drove to Macy's.

Macy and I hadn't talked much the day before, and when we did, she had shared surprisingly little with me about her visit with Noel's mother, other than her obvious disappointment. I didn't press her.

I told her that I suspected that Mrs. Thorup wasn't being entirely truthful when she said Noel didn't live there. What college student from a well-off family doesn't come home for Thanksgiving? I suggested to Macy that she go back again and refuse to leave until she saw her sister. I even offered to go with her. But she just changed the topic.

I arrived at Macy's a little past one. Macy's car was gone, and the walk and porch were covered with snow nearly three inches deep, including where Macy's car had been. Wherever she'd gone, she'd been gone for a while. I knocked on the door and Joette answered. She wore an apron over her Levi's and a T-shirt, and I felt a bit overdressed. She looked happy to see me. She also looked a little tired.

"Hi, Mark. Happy Thanksgiving. Come on in." She sounded like Bob Barker saying "Come on down!" to *The Price Is Right* contestants.

"Happy Thanksgiving," I returned. "I thought I'd shovel your driveway first. Do you have a snow shovel?"

"You don't have to do that."

"It's getting pretty deep."

"Thank you. I just don't have the energy I used to. The shovel's inside the little shed there. Just let yourself in when you're done."

It took me more than a half hour to clear the driveway and front walk. I had expected Macy to return before I finished, but she didn't. I kicked my feet against the concrete step to clear the snow from my shoes, and then let myself in. Joette had put a rug down for me; I stomped my feet some more before I finally decided to just take off my shoes.

The home was a joyful assault on the senses. Cheerful Christmas music wafted from the kitchen, accompanied by the pleasant smells of baking—hot rolls, sweet potatoes, turkey and a few things I couldn't identify but knew I liked. I breathed it all in. It had been some time since I had smelled anything that good.

I took my coat off and lay it across the couch, then I walked back into the kitchen. Joette was whipping potatoes with a hand mixer. She looked up as I entered. "Thanks for doing that."

"No problem. It smells wonderful in here. Like home."

"That's a nice compliment. Macy and I like to cook."

"Where is Macy?"

"She's still at the shelter."

She said this as if I knew, or should know, what she was talking about. "The shelter?"

"The homeless shelter down on Third South. She goes down every year to help out on Thanksgiving."

"That's really . . . noble." I said. *Dumb*

word, I thought. I was still nervous around Joette.

"Well, you know Macy. Always saving the world. But she does it for herself too. She once ate dinner at that shelter. I think that going back is a chance for her to keep track of how far she's come."

"She credits you for that."

Joette smiled at this. "We help each other."

I leaned back against the counter. "What can I help with?"

"Can you carve the turkey?"

"Sure."

The bird was on the counter next to the oven, covered with foil. I looked around for a knife. Joette gestured with a toss of her head. "Use the carving knife in that block over there. You can put the meat on that serving plate."

"Got it."

Joette went back to whipping potatoes. When she finished, she took the beaters from the bowl and ran a finger along the bowl's mouth and licked her finger like she was eating frosting. She popped the beaters off and set them in the sink.

"You know, Thanksgiving is Macy's and my anniversary."

"Anniversary?"

"The anniversary of our first day living together. It's our little joke: she came for Thanksgiving dinner and never left." She took the bowl of potatoes over to another counter. She came back with a cake pan of unbaked rolls and began brushing them with butter. "So I'm sure Macy filled you in about meeting Noel's mother."

"Some. It's too bad. Do you think she'll keep looking for her sister?"

"I think she will someday, when she's absolutely sure it is right for Noel." She took a can opener from a drawer and opened a can of cranberry sauce. She dumped the red gelatin onto a plate and threw the can away, then licked her fingers again. "I think she already has a lot to process just with finding her father."

"I think you're right." I carved into the side of the turkey, revealing a steaming white flank. I speared it with a fork and laid it on the pewter serving plate.

"So how's *your* father doing?" she asked.

I was a little embarrassed by the question. "I don't know." I cut another slice of turkey. "We don't really talk."

"Macy said you don't get along real well with your father."

"We don't get along at all."

"Do you mind if I ask why?"

I wasn't certain that I wanted to have this conversation. "We have a lot of history."

"History's about the past, right?"

I was now certain that I didn't want to have this conversation. Joette leaned back against the counter.

"I have a father story," she said. "My mother died when I was fourteen. My father never remarried. So he was both dad and mom to me. Some part of me always resented not having a mother. I think that in some bizarre way I blamed him for her death—as if he could have stopped it somehow. It sounds foolish now, but teenagers don't think about much but themselves. At least I didn't.

"And then one day I had this epiphany. I realized that being a parent was like being the Wizard of Oz."

I remembered what Macy had said earlier about Joette's life philosophy and I had to hide my amusement. "What do you mean?"

"You know the part when Dorothy and her friends go to see the Wizard? This big, ominous head talks to them and they're all terrified. Then her dog . . ."

"Toto," I said.

"Right. Toto pulls back the curtain and there's a little man behind it pulling levers and throwing switches. And he says into his microphone, 'Ignore the man behind the curtain.' I think that being a parent is like being the man behind the curtain. We pretend that we know what we're doing—that we're omnipotent and all-knowing—when the truth is we're just back behind the curtain throwing levers and switches, doing the best we can."

In spite of myself, I found her explanation interesting. "And then our kids find out that we're not as great as they thought we were?"

"Exactly. And then they're angry and disappointed that we can't meet their expectations—as unrealistic as they are."

"So did you and your father get along better after you learned this?"

She frowned. "Well, actually, by that time it was too late. He passed on eleven years after my mother died. I never really thanked him for all he did for me." She suddenly smiled. "He tried so hard. You should see the prom dress he bought for me. He didn't want any boys to get the wrong idea about me so he picked out a dress for me himself. The collar practically went up to my ears. I put it on at home, then after my date picked me up, we went to my friend's house and I borrowed one of her dresses. I didn't think about what I'd done until I was in the middle of showing him my prom pictures. I'm not sure if he didn't notice or if he just didn't want to make a fuss. But he sacrificed to get me that dress. I regret what I did to this day."

A buzzer went off. "Pies," she said. She put on oven mitts and brought two pies from the oven, a pumpkin pie and a lattice-crusted apple pie sprinkled with cinnamon-sugar.

"I love pie," I said.

"Good. Because there's plenty." She brought out another pan with small strips of baked crust sprinkled with sugar. "Here's something to snack on." Joette washed her hands. "I'm going to go clean up. Just make yourself at home. You know where the TV is."

"Thanks."

I took several pieces of crust cookies, then went into the living room and turned on a football game. Macy returned within the hour. I stood as she entered and we kissed. "Happy Thanksgiving," she said.

"It is now," I replied. I helped her off with her coat.

"Where's Jo?"

"She went to change."

"I'm right here," Joette said, walking into the room.

"I'm sorry I'm so late. They were really short-handed this year. It took us that long to serve everybody."

"We're okay," Joette said. "So how was it?"

"It was good. It's always good," Macy said. "So what's left to do?"

"Just set the table."

"We've got it," Macy said. "C'mon, Mark."

The table was small and a leaf in the middle changed it from a circle to an oval. Setting the table only took a few minutes. We carried in everything but the pies and then sat down to eat.

"I'll pray," Joette said.

We bowed our heads. Macy reached over

and took Joette's hand, then mine. Joette reached over and took my other hand, completing the circle.

"Dear Lord. We are grateful for the many blessings we have. For our home and food and clothing." She paused and her voice faltered with emotion. "Especially for the time we have together. Let us be thankful not just today, but always. Amen."

"Amen."

I reached for a roll.

"Wait," Macy said.

I stopped, my fingers an inch from the breadbasket. I looked at her.

"Before we eat everyone has to say something they're thankful for. Mark, you're the guest. You go first."

Both women looked at me expectantly.

"Okay," I said, retracting my hand. "Well, for one, I'm grateful that you invited me to share today with you. And I'm very grateful that Macy came into my life when she did."

Macy smiled broadly. "Thank you. And you're welcome." She turned to Joette. "Now it's your turn."

"I'm grateful for many, many things. I'm grateful that Mark is here with us. And most of all, I'm grateful for that Thanksgiving Day five years ago when Macy came for dinner and never left." She reached over and squeezed Macy's hand, then Macy leaned back in her chair.

"Okay. I'm thankful that I've had both of you help me through the last three weeks. It's been a pretty emotional ride. And even though things didn't turn out the way I hoped they would, I learned something very important." She paused, suddenly overcome by emotion. "That all I was really looking for was home. And I have a home, thanks to Jo. And I have a new friend. And I have a roof over my head—that's always a good thing. I really have a lot to be thankful for."

"Amen," Joette said.

"Amen," I repeated.

Macy turned to Joette. "Remember last week when you asked me what I wanted for Christmas?"

Joette nodded. "You came up with something?"

"I've finally decided."

"This sounds serious. Should I get a notepad?"

Macy laughed. "No. I just want one thing." She looked at her and was suddenly nervous. "I can't believe I'm afraid to ask now."

"Don't worry," Joette said, "I'm not afraid to say 'no.' "

"That's what *I'm* afraid of." Macy took a breath then blurted out, "I want you to legally adopt me. I want to be your daughter."

For a moment Joette said nothing. Then she began to cry. She stood up from her chair, and Macy stood and they wrapped their arms around each other. It was a few minutes before Joette could speak. "It would be the greatest honor of my life."

"Thank you," Macy said. "Thank you, thank you."

After a few more minutes of their laughing and crying, I said, "Can I eat?"

They both turned to me and laughed. "Men," Macy said. "Always putting their stomachs before their hearts."

✦

The meal was every bit as wonderful as it looked and smelled. It may not have been southern, but it was pretty darn good. When we finished dessert, Macy brought us steaming cups of mint truffle hot chocolate. Joette was the first up from the table. She carried a small stack of dishes to the sink. When she turned on the water, Macy jumped up from her seat. "We'll do the dishes, Jo. You've slaved enough for one day. Go rest."

Joette looked grateful for the offer. "Are you sure?"

"We got it," I said, also rising.

"Okay." Joette disappeared down the hallway.

When her door shut, I said, "She looked tired."

"I know. She hasn't been feeling well lately. I keep telling her to see a doctor, but she keeps insisting that there's nothing wrong."

*

Macy and I did the dishes, then, at her suggestion, we put on our coats and went out for a walk. The snow had not stopped falling and the street was white and silent. There's something magically calming about the peace of new snow. I took Macy's hand as we walked and she held mine tightly. I wanted to talk to her about us, about our future, but I suddenly felt fearful. Instead, I said, "I'm so full I can hardly walk. Everything was great."

"It turned out well. It's been a nice day, hasn't it?"

"All of it. Especially when you asked Joette to adopt you. You made her so happy."

"I was really afraid to ask her. I didn't know what she'd say."

I knew exactly how she felt. "It was perfect," I said.

She sighed pleasantly. "It was, wasn't it? I've thought about this for a long time. I guess the clincher was when one of my coworkers told me that when his parents were killed in a plane crash his grandparents became his legal guardians. I realized that if I ever had children and something happened to me, Irene Hummel might be given custody. There's no way I would let that happen." She turned and looked at me. "You realize that means I'll have had three last names." She rolled her eyes. "I'm twenty-one years old and I've had three last names."

"You know, I've been thinking about that very thing."

"Really?"

"Well, I was wondering what you'd think of making it four."

She looked at me quizzically. "Making what four?"

"Your last name."

She continued to look at me as if I were speaking Chinese. "What do you mean?"

"I mean . . . getting married."

She laughed nervously. "Well, I'm sure when that day comes, I'll be okay with it."

"I mean now."

She stopped walking and looked at me with an expression I couldn't read. "Are you serious?"

"Yes."

"You're asking me to marry you?"

"Yes."

She just stared at me for a moment, then she turned and began walking back toward the house

"Macy."

Her pace quickened. When I caught up to her, I saw that she was crying. I stepped in front of her, blocking her path. She had covered her eyes with one hand and wouldn't look at me. Her hand was trembling.

"I just asked you to marry me."

"I know."

I took her hand and gently pulled it away. She looked up at me, her face wet from tears. "Why are you doing this?"

Her question baffled me as much as the rest of her reaction. "Because I love you."

"How can you say that? You don't really know me."

"Of course I know you. We've been through so much together."

She just shook her head.

"I know it's only been three weeks, but I'm absolutely sure that I want to spend the rest of my life with you. Sometimes you just know these things."

"There are things in my past. Dark things you don't know about."

"I don't care about your past. It's your future, *our* future, that I'm thinking about."

"There's no difference. The past *is* our future."

"That's not true. We can transcend our past."

"Have you?"

Her question stopped me.

"Mark, what if you're really just trying to fill the hole in your life that your mother left when she died?"

"I'm not," I said.

"Really? You don't talk about her, or the rest of your family. You haven't gone home. And your anger toward your father . . ." She looked at me and wiped her eyes. "I'm not running from my past, Mark, and I can't share my future with someone who's running from his." She looked down and turned away from me. "I've got to go."

She ran back to the house. I just stood there dumbfounded and clueless as I watched her disappear with my heart.

CHAPTER

Twenty-five

It's time for me to face the truth.
Time to start burning bridges.

✦ MARK SMART'S DIARY ✦

I felt like my heart had been run over by a cement truck. I went home and picked up my guitar, but not even playing brought me relief. I called Macy's house four times that night. The first three times I called, no one answered. The fourth time Joette picked up. Her voice was solemn. "Hi, Mark, it's Jo."

"Is Macy there?"

"She's already in bed."

"Is she asleep?"

She hesitated. "I'm afraid that she doesn't want to talk to you."

I took a deep breath. "You mean like right now or for the rest of her life?"

"I'm sorry about this, Mark. You might want to give her a day or two. She's pretty upset."

I exhaled. "Was I completely stupid to think she might consider marrying me?"

Her voice lightened. "I don't think so. I don't think she thinks so either."

"Fooled me," I said. I sighed again. "Two days."

"Two days. She'll probably be ready to talk by then."

✷

As difficult as it was, I didn't call the house for the next two days. On Sunday, I called three times, all without success. I tried again Monday morning, but still no one answered. With each call I grew more upset and my heartbreak began to be tempered by anger. Then my anger turned to doubt. How could she dispose of me so easily? Maybe she was right. *Maybe I didn't really know her.*

I called every day that week, but she never answered. Then I stopped calling, hoping that she might call me. I guess, like all faithless, I was looking for some kind of sign, but none was forthcoming. Nine days after Thanksgiving, I accepted that for reasons I didn't understand, Macy was done with me. I also came to the conclusion that there was no reason for me to stay in Salt Lake City. At the rate I was saving money, it would take me years to get back in school.

It was time to face reality. Coming to Utah was a mistake. It was time to go home.

The first thing I did was quit my job. It wasn't hard. I think my coworkers envied me, especially Victor, who asked if I'd sell him my Malibu. We agreed on a price and that he'd take possession the day I left. Next, I gave up my apartment. I'm pretty sure that my landlord was glad when I told him that I was leaving. Actually, I'm surprised he didn't break open a bottle of champagne. It took him all of a half hour to hang out a vacancy sign. I took some of what little money I had saved and purchased a one-way airline ticket for Huntsville.

Wednesday was my last day at work. It was around eleven when I said goodbye to my coworkers, and though I'd promised myself that I wouldn't chase her, I found myself driving to the Hut. Macy was working at the front counter and looked up as I entered. Just seeing her brought me a stew of emotions: relief, anger, sadness, fear. From her expression I suspect she felt much the same.

"Hi," I said.

"Hey."

"How you doing?"

She just kind of tossed her head.

"I've been trying to call you."

"I'm sorry."

I just looked at her. "That's it?"

She nodded.

My heart sank even more. I took a deep breath. "I just came to thank you for everything you've done for me. I owe you."

"You don't owe me."

Another worker interrupted us. "Mary, the phone's for you."

"Take a message, please."

"It's Jeff."

"Tell him I'll call him back."

Macy turned back to me.

"And in spite of how everything turned out," I continued, "I'm really glad I got to know you. I'm sorry that I ruined everything." I took another deep breath. "I just wanted to say goodbye before I left."

She flinched. "Where are you going?"

"Home."

"For how long?"

I shrugged. "I bought a one-way ticket."

She looked at me in disbelief. "When are you leaving?"

"Saturday. This Saturday."

She was speechless. It was almost like pressing the reset button on a computer and watching for it to reboot. Finally, I said, "I better let you go. Give Jo my best."

"I'll do that."

A lump rose in my throat. "Well, take care."

"You too."

I walked out of the café. My eyes moistened as I headed out to my car. I couldn't believe that after all we'd been through, it had ended like this.

CHAPTER
Twenty-six

Joette called this morning to set up a meeting, presumably to talk about Macy. There was something in her voice that makes me think that all is not well in Oz.

✦ MARK SMART'S DIARY ✦

The next morning I was teaching my last guitar lesson when my landlord knocked on the door.

"Phone's for you," he said, sounding less annoyed than usual. I think knowing that I would soon be gone made him nicer.

"Who is it?"

"A woman. She says it's important."

"Thanks."

I left my student practicing a chord and went up to my landlord's apartment. I picked up the phone. "Hello."

"Mark, this is Joette."

"Hey, what's up?"

"I was wondering if we could get together and talk."

"Sure, but it will have to be soon. I'm leaving Saturday."

"I know, Macy told me. Could we get together tomorrow, during my lunch break? I'll treat you to lunch."

"Denny's, right?"

"On State and Twenty-First."

"What time?"

"My lunch break's not until two."

"I'll be there. How's Macy?"

She paused. "We'll talk about that."

C H A P T E R
Twenty-seven

How foolish to believe we have any idea of what is really going on around us or that permanency is an earthly option.

✦ MARK SMART'S DIARY ✦

Joette was waiting for me in a corner booth when I arrived. She was wearing her waitress uniform and was drinking cola from a straw. She waved me over and I sat down across from her. "Thanks for coming. It's good to see you."

"You too."

"How have you been?"

"I've been better."

"I know." She handed me a menu. "Are you hungry?"

"I was born hungry."

She grinned. "Then let's order first." I opened the menu and looked through it. When I set it down, she asked, "Ready?"

"I'll have the Reuben."

"Good choice," she said, sounding very much the waitress she was. "With the fries or salad?"

"Fries."

"And what do you want to drink?"

"I'll have a Coke."

"Okay." She walked back to the kitchen. I looked around the restaurant; this was Joette's world. She returned just a few minutes later carrying my drink. She set it down in front of me and slid into her seat. Her expression turned grave.

"I need to ask you something very important."

"Okay."

"How do you feel about Macy?"

Under the circumstances I thought this was a strange question. "You know I asked her to marry me."

"I know," she said, "but how do you feel now?"

"Hurt. Angry." I took a deep breath. "And I wake up every morning with a heartache. She's all I think about."

"If you could have her back, would you take her?"

"Of course. But that's really not my decision."

"Macy is hurting too. She misses you. Maybe even more than she knows. But she's afraid, and she has every right to be. If you had lived through what she has, you'd be afraid too."

I slowly rotated my cup in my hands. "Yeah, so what do I do?"

"Please don't give up on her. She's going to need you."

There was something about the way Joette said this that made me anxious. "What do you mean . . . ? "

She lifted her napkin and dabbed at her eyes. "Sorry." She exhaled deeply. "Do you believe that people come into our lives for a reason?"

"I don't know. My mother always said that. Maybe she was right. Look how Macy came into mine. She saved my life."

"I know what you mean. When I first met Macy, I thought I was there to save her. Five years later I realized that she came to save me."

"What do you mean?"

She looked at me thoughtfully. "Macy came into my life about twelve weeks after I lost my little girl. Angela was only four years old. My husband was out of town at the time, as he usually was. He was a sales rep for a medical oxygen supply company, and he was always on the road. I was used to doing things alone with Angela. She had seen someone roasting hot dogs on TV and she wanted to do it too, so I took her up into the canyons for a weenie roast. I was trying to start the fire, and Angela was sitting on a blanket not ten feet from me. I was never much of an outdoorsman and I had trouble getting the fire going, but I finally did. When I turned around, Angela was gone. I ran around, screaming for her, but I couldn't find her anywhere. It was spring and the creek was nearly overflowing its banks. I was afraid she might have walked too close to the water and fallen in." Joette lifted her napkin to her eyes again. "The next day park rangers found her little body a mile down the creek."

"I'm so sorry."

She breathed in deeply. "I can't tell you what a nightmare that time was. I had to call my husband and tell him that she was missing, and the next morning I had to call him and tell him she was dead. He completely blamed me. The one person whose support I needed more than any other turned on me. I had a breakdown and spent five weeks in the university psychiatric ward. When they released me, my psychologist told me to go back to work—to get my life going again. I did. I was heavily tranquilized. I felt like the Tin Man, heartless and hollow, just going through the motions. I worked twelve hours a day, then went home and cried until I slept. Then I'd get up the next morning and do the same thing.

"I'd see my counselor every week, but deep inside I knew I wasn't going to make it. It was like I could hear this train in the distance coming to take me away. Every day it got a little bit closer. It was pretty close to my stop when one day this sweet girl shows up to bus tables at work. She was so young; I thought she was a child, but she acted much older than she looked. And she worked hard. I didn't know her story, but there was a lot of talk about her among the other waitresses. I noticed that she only had a few outfits. I'm sure she sensed that something was wrong with me, but she never said anything. She would just smile, and she always had a cheerful word. She made sure my tables were watered, and got cleared first. She was a waitress's dream.

"One night, the day before Thanksgiving, near the end of my shift, this guy came in with a little girl. She looked just like *my* little girl. I tried not to look at her. While they were ordering, he called her Angela. I took their order then went back to the kitchen and collapsed. I was sitting there on the floor crying. No one knew what to do. Except Macy. She got on the floor with me and put her arms around me, and even though she didn't know why I was crying, she held me. She took the order out to the man and his daughter and took care of my tables until I was able to pull myself together.

"After my shift we went out to my car and just talked.

"I couldn't believe the insight this young woman had. Or maybe it was just that she was willing to listen. When we finished talking, it was probably three in the morning. I knew that she usually walked home, so I asked if I could give her a ride. Even though we were in my car, she refused. She didn't want to tell me where she lived. It took a while but I finally got her to admit that she was living at the homeless shelter about a mile down the street. I invited her to come home with me."

The love Joette felt for Macy was evident in her eyes. "That was five years ago. I guess we just got so busy living together that the train just passed me by." She smiled at me. "So you and I have something in common. I thought I was saving Macy when the opposite was true. You thought Macy was sent here to save you. I think it's also the other way around."

"I don't understand."

"I don't think it's a coincidence that you showed up when you did." Then she looked into my eyes. "I'm dying, Mark."

"What?"

"Macy told you that I had cancer."

I nodded. "She said you had it in your eye."

"Ocular melanoma. And she also told you that it's in remission."

"Right."

"It was. But it's come back. And it's stage four."

"What does that mean?"

"In my case it means the cancer has metastasized to my liver."

I just looked at her in disbelief. "How bad is that?"

"Pretty much as bad as it gets. I'm out of options—no surgery, no chemo. They just sent me home and told me to get my affairs in order."

I was stunned. "How long?"

"A few months. Maybe less."

For a moment I was speechless. My mouth went dry. "But Macy thinks you're fine."

"Macy just thinks I'm sick and should see a doctor. She doesn't know I've seen too many of them."

"Why haven't you told her?"

"Because I was waiting."

"For what?"

"For you."

I looked at her quizzically. "For me?"

"I prayed that God would send someone to take my place. I think He sent you."

I didn't speak for a moment. Another waitress walked up carrying our orders. "There's your Cobb, Jo. And for your cute friend, a Reuben. Can I get you anything else?"

"No. Thanks, Emily."

"Enjoy."

Joette turned back to me. I didn't even look at my food. "I take it they don't know either."

She shook her head. "Not yet." She leaned back. "You know, Mark, the longer I live, the more I see a pattern to our lives. The universe is a trillion, trillion threads moving in seemingly unrelated directions. Yet when you look at them together, they create a remarkable tapestry. You think she saved you. She did. But that's so you could save her."

I looked at my cup, unsure of what to say.

Finally I asked, "When are you going to tell her?"

"I don't know. But I can't wait much longer. It's already obvious I'm not well. In another week or two I'll have to quit work. That's why I wanted to make sure you were still around."

"She won't take my calls . . ."

"She loves you, Mark. She's fighting it, but she does. To get through to her it's going to take a lot of faith on your part—enough for both of you. Macy's greatest hurts have come from those who were closest to her. She wants to get close to you. But think of the risk that poses to her. Everything inside of her tells her to run. It's self-preservation. And that's a pretty powerful instinct."

"How do you break through that?"

She looked at me for a moment and I saw the answer in her eyes. "With love. Unconditional, unrelenting love."

I breathed in deeply. It was a few moments before I spoke. "I fly back to Alabama this Saturday."

"Are you coming back?"

I shook my head. "I wasn't planning to. I've pretty much shut down my life here."

Her face showed her disappointment. "I hope that you'll reconsider. Macy's worth it."

"I'll think about it. I promise."

"Fair enough," she said. "I'm adopting Macy on Friday. It would mean a lot to the both of us if you could be there."

"I'll be there."

"Thank you. Now eat, before your sandwich gets cold."

We didn't say much as we ate. I had lost my appetite and ate more out of obligation than hunger. On a napkin she wrote out the time and place of the adoption. When I was finished, we went out to the parking lot. Joette walked me to my car. "Thank you for talking with me. And whatever you decide, I appreciate all you've done for us."

I unlocked my car door. "I do love her, Joette."

"I know. And I love you for that." We hugged.

When we parted, I said, "I'm sorry that you're sick."

Her eyes filled. "Me too."

On the drive home I turned on the radio to an FM station that played all Christmas music. A saxophone played *Silent Night.* As I listened, I began to cry for a good woman I had just met and was about to lose.

CHAPTER
Twenty-eight

The attorney handling Macy's adoption asked if she wanted copies of the final adoption papers sent to Irene Hummel. Macy didn't see the point in it. Revenge is only for those still chained.

✦ MARK SMART'S DIARY ✦

Friday morning I woke with a headache. I think my body was reacting to the stress of seeing Macy and the truth be known, I didn't want to go through that again. It didn't matter. I had already made a commitment to Joette and nothing short of being in a coma would keep me from going.

Even though Macy was an adult, the women still needed to hire an attorney and go through the regular adoption process. The only thing not required was a permission form from the Hummels and home study—something experience had given Macy very little confidence in anyway. Joette knew several attorneys who were among her regulars at Denny's, and one of them offered to do the legal work for her pro bono.

The adoption was set for noon at the Salt Lake County Courthouse—the courthouse where Macy had been adopted by the Hummels thirteen years earlier. When I arrived,

Macy, Joette and their attorney were already there, reading through the paperwork.

A police officer stood near the vacant judge's bench, and there were a dozen or so other people in the courtroom who looked to be friends of Macy and Joette's. I walked in and sat down near the back of the room. Joette noticed me and waved. Macy turned and looked at me and she also waved, though there was sadness in her eyes. I mouthed, "Good luck," and she mouthed back, "Thank you."

The judge arrived a few minutes later and everyone in the room rose. Macy and Joette were asked to approach the bench and sit on the side that defendants would normally sit on. Then, at the judge's beckoning, Macy and Joette entered through a swinging gate and sat down in front of the judge's desk. He was an older man, bald and wearing a smile nearly as wide as his face.

"Well, young ladies, I thought I'd seen everything in this courtroom, but I've never before had the pleasure of presiding over a proceeding such as this one. Under the circumstances, I think it would be appropriate for the two of you to give testimony as to why, at this later age of life, you want to have this adoption take place."

Neither of the women was expecting to speak, but Joette quickly raised her hand.

"Your honor, I'd like to speak first."

"By all means."

As she stood, she suddenly teared up. Macy rubbed her back. Joette raised her hand to her breast and took a deep breath. "When I lost my only child, I was sure no one could ever take her place or heal my heart. I couldn't imagine ever feeling joy again.

"I was partially right. No one could take her place. But someone did heal my heart. This beautiful young lady seated next to me. I believe that God sent this angel to me. She has given me a reason to live. When she asked if I would be willing to adopt her, I think that hole in my heart was finally filled. Your honor, in my heart Macy is already my daughter. But it would be a great privilege to have the world recognize her as my daughter as well. Thank you."

Joette sat down next to Macy and they hugged. Everyone else in the room was smiling or crying. The judge beamed.

Then Macy stood, wiping tears back from

her eyes. "Thirteen years ago I was brought to this very building to be adopted by a family that didn't love me and I didn't want to be a part of. I think it's appropriate that the room I was adopted in is right behind this one. Because as of today it is all behind me. Today I come of my own choice to be legally bound as a daughter to a woman I love and want to belong to. This woman has done more than give me a place to live; she has taught me the meaning of love and family and home." She turned to Joette. "I guess it's never too late to find a home."

For a moment the two women just looked at each other. Then Macy turned back to the judge. "Thank you, your honor." She sat down next to Joette and held her. I knew Macy still didn't know how ill Joette really was, and it was hard to control my emotions. The judge was obviously touched by the women's words. "Are there any objections to this proceeding?" he asked, though I was pretty sure he'd toss his gavel at anyone who did. The only responses were a few random headshakes, whispered "nos" and one loud "Heck no".

"Very well, by the authority vested in me by the state of Utah, I hereby grant this adoption. Congratulations to both of you, and may God bless."

Macy and Joette rose and the whole of the spectators descended upon them. I walked up as well, straggling a bit behind the others. When I got near to Joette, she threw her arms around me.

"Thank you so much for coming."

"Congratulations," I said. "You have a new girl."

Joette just beamed. Macy was talking to someone else and I turned to go, when she excused herself and ran to me. She took my hand and I turned around to face her.

"Thanks for coming," she said.

"You're welcome. Congratulations."

For a moment we just looked at each other. She looked down and swallowed. "I don't want you to leave."

I looked down, avoiding her eyes.

"There's nothing here for me," I said.

She looked back up, and I could see the pain my statement caused her. She bowed her head and lifted her hand to cover her eyes. I put my arms around her and pulled her into my chest, and she began to sob. It was painful seeing her hurt. It was also painful being this close to someone I loved and couldn't have. Still, in a twisted sort of way, something inside of me was glad. After a week of solitary suffering, I was tired of being the only one hurting over all this. But in the end I couldn't enjoy whatever perverse pleasure I was feeling, because I didn't want to see her in pain. More proof that I really did love her. After a few minutes I kissed the top of her head.

"Good luck, Mace. You take care of yourself."

She stepped back from me and looked me in the eyes. I have never had anyone look deeper into my soul. Still, as difficult as it was, I took a deep breath and turned from her. She was quickly surrounded by people who were happy for her and who thought they knew why she was crying.

C H A P T E R
Twenty-nine

I have learned first hand that one well-placed truth can counter a lifetime of ignorance.

✦ MARK SMART'S DIARY ✦

Saturday morning as the sun peeked over the Wasatch Range, I picked Victor up and we drove to the airport. Even though I pushed thoughts of Macy from my mind, there were reminders everywhere I looked. *How could we have created so much history in such a brief time?* I wondered. For the first time since I met him, Victor's conversation actually concerned something pertinent to the real world. He wanted to know why I was going back to Alabama. I couldn't really answer him. Or maybe I just didn't want to. "It's just time," I said.

He had already paid me for my car, and he dropped me off curbside at the Delta terminal. I pulled my two bags from the trunk. We said goodbye and he drove off in my Malibu. I curb-checked my bags, shoved my boarding pass into my shirt pocket and went inside the terminal to wait.

My flight took me from Salt Lake City International through Atlanta's Hartsfield with a three-hour layover. I had plenty of time to think. Macy was right about one thing: in the last four weeks I had thought little about my mother. It was not that she was forgettable; it was rather that I was afraid of where those thoughts might take me. Now, as I prepared to face my loss head-on, I realized how distant I really was from home. I didn't even know where my mother was buried. I called my Aunt Marge from the Atlanta airport and told her that I was coming home. She was elated at the news and offered to pick me up at the airport, but I turned her down. I needed time alone. I did accept her offer to stay at her house. That way my father would never even know I was in town. Not that he'd care.

I landed in Huntsville around 6 P.M. Maybe sixteen minutes past. I carried my bags, then walked directly out of the terminal and hailed a cab. The driver seemed a little perplexed by my destination.

"I'm taking you to the city cemetery?"

"Yes, sir."

He shrugged. "Okay."

The cab dropped me and my luggage off and, at my request, left. My aunt had told me the approximate location of my mother's grave in the cemetery. I wasn't really sure how I'd get to my aunt's house; I just knew I didn't want anyone around.

It was snowing lightly, and there was more snow on the ground than I ever remembered having in Huntsville—nothing compared to Salt Lake City—but enough to make walking difficult. I hid my bags behind a hedge, then trudged in ankle-deep snow between the stones, scanning the names. I searched for nearly twenty minutes without luck and began to wonder if I had misunderstood the directions my aunt had given me. I was walking back toward my bags when I found these words carved into rose granite:

Alice Liddel Smart
Beloved Wife and Mother
June 16, 1946—October 23, 1988

Only at that moment did my mother's death become fully real to me. I fell to my knees and began to cry. Then, in anguish, I shouted, "Mom," the word muffled in the quiet, snow-draped setting. I fell forward to my hands, and my body heaved while the snow collected on and around me. I didn't brush it away. I wanted it to cover me, to bury me with her—"Why did you leave, Mom?"

The winter sun was beginning to wane, leaving the cemetery chill and in shadows. I knelt there motionless and cold as the stone in front of me.

I don't know how long I'd been there before I heard the sound of footsteps crunching through the snow. I looked to see who it was. It was Stu. I stood up and he stopped walking. We just stared at each other. He stood about twenty feet from me wearing his oil-stained navy blue mechanic's jacket, the one with the patch with his name sewed on it. I was angry at him for trespassing on my grief.

"How did you know I was here?"

"Marge told me."

Now I was angry at her as well.

"How you been?" he asked.

"Since when do you care how I've been?"

He just looked at me with a hollow stare. There was no anger in his gaze—at that moment I had a monopoly on anger. "I'll tell you how I'm doing. I lost my mother, two girls and my scholarship to school. I've been cleaning toilets to get by. But I'm sure that makes you happy."

He rubbed his face. "No. It don't."

As much as I wanted to leave, I suppose, in my own way, I was finally standing my ground. "Why did you come?"

"I wanted to see you."

"Why?"

He couldn't answer. He sniffed and looked around. Then he looked down at his feet. After a while he said, "I was afraid I might never see you again."

He was right. I hadn't intended on ever seeing him again. Still his reply surprised me. "You spent your whole life chasing me away, and now you're afraid I might not come back?"

"I guess so."

I didn't know what was going through his mind, but I knew that this was likely my only chance to say what needed to be said.

"So why did you have to make everything so hard? Why couldn't you have been a real father?"

I expected him to lash out at me, but he just stood there looking at me sadly. He took a deep breath. "Alright. Come with me. It's time you knew."

"Knew what?"

"I want to show you somethin'." He began walking away from me, unsteadily in the snow. At first I just stood there, not sure of what he was up to. Then curiosity prevailed. I followed him, always staying at least ten yards back. The only noise was the wind and the crisp sound of our steps in the crusted snow. Finally he stopped at the base of a knoll at another headstone, his hands in his pockets.

The headstone was alabaster, weather-stained and partially concealed in shadow, capped with a thin layer of icy snow. Still keeping my distance from Stu, I walked up to it, my eyes focused on the words etched into its face. The stone had an American flag engraved on it.

Virgil Marcus Hunt
February 14, 1949—March 4, 1969

I looked at him, expecting an explanation, but he said nothing. Finally I asked, "Who's this?"

My father said nothing. He just rubbed his hand through his hair like he always did when he was at a loss for words.

"Why did you bring me here?"

He turned and looked at me with an anguished expression. "It's your father."

"What?"

He began walking away from the grave as if it was painful to be near it. I followed him.

He didn't stop walking until he reached my mother's grave. He sat down on a white marble bench a few yards away and buried his face in his hands.

"What do you mean, *my father?*"

It seemed a long time before he looked up. "I'm sure it crossed your mind more than a few times how a woman like your mother ended up with a guy like me. I wasn't your mother's first choice. Never was. She was dating a couple fellas. Me and Virgil back there, and some other boy from Birmingham. But Virgil was her favorite. He was a student at the university and a real BMOC. He played the guitar real well. I was just . . . you know. No surprise she chose him.

"While they was still engaged, he was drafted. They hurried and eloped, didn't tell no one. I think I was about the last to know. One day when I thought maybe I still had a chance with her, I went to get her flowers at Pat's, and the girl there knew Alice. Told me

Alice and Virgil was married. She'd made up the bridal bouquet herself. That about killed me. Girl behind the counter at the florist shop knew and I didn't.

"Six weeks later Virgil left for Vietnam. Lots of boys we knew didn't come home. He was killed just four months there. Just like that. Your mother barely nineteen and she was a widow." He turned and looked at me. "And she was pregnant with you.

"When I heard he was killed, I come back around, to give my condolences, but we both knew why I was there. She was grievin' pretty sore, but she didn't turn me away." He looked down. "I shouldn't have stayed. I knew her heart was still with him, but I didn't love no one else. Next thing I know, we was courtin'. I was pretty sure she just wanted her child to have a father—couple times she nearly said as much.

"I told myself it didn't matter. Hearts do that. A chance for a guy like me to be with Alice—that's like winnin' the Alabama and Florida lottery all at once—who cares how you get it. I told myself with time she'd come around to love me." Suddenly my father's eyes welled up with tears. "She never did. She put up with me. But she never loved me. It was like she'd already given away that part of her heart."

For the first time in my life, I saw my father cry. He looked at me the whole time, unashamed of the tears streaming down his face. "I loved her, son. I would've been anything she wanted. But I couldn't be *who* she wanted. She wanted that man back there." His voice cracked. "She loved you something fierce. And I was jealous of you and of that love. Because I knew it was more than just you was her boy. It was 'cause you was a part a him."

He wiped his eyes with the back of his hand. "I know I wasn't good to you. I ain't proud of it. I took all my hurt out on you. It wasn't right, it was just what it was."

He put his hands into his coat pockets and looked back at the stone. "That's why I came. I wanted to tell you how sorry I was." He looked up at me and into my eyes. "I'm sorry."

In my twenty years of life I had never heard my father speak those two words. Neither of us spoke for some time. The snow still fell, shrouding us. Then he brought something out of his coat pocket.

"Anyway, seeing how I'll probably never see you again, I brought you some things."

He stood and walked to me. Then he reached out his hand. I put mine out and he dropped a gold ring into my palm.

"That was your mother's wedding ring from Virgil. She wore it on a chain around her neck. Never took it off. I know she'd want you to have it. I hope you don't mind, but I kept the chain."

I lifted the ring to examine it. It was a yellow gold band with a marquise diamond surrounded by small chips of dark blue sapphires. I remembered that I had seen the ring once when she was weeding the flower bed and it fell outside her blouse. I asked her about it, but she just stowed it back inside her shirt and continued pulling weeds.

I put the ring in my pocket. Then Stu brought out of his coat a larger packet, a brown paper lunch sack smudged with motor oil. He handed it to me. I opened the bag and looked inside. It was a large stack of bills, mostly twenties and fifties.

"What's this?"

"It's money I'd been puttin' away for your schoolin'. I know you'll do real well, whatever you end up doing. You was always real smart like your mom. And your dad."

I could tell it was difficult for him to say that last word. Then he turned and began to walk away, shuffling slowly through the snow. I don't really know how, but at that moment Stuart Smart was no longer the icon I had hated and feared. He was just a man—hurting and human. A man like me. He was what Joette said, *the man behind the curtain.* He began disappearing in the shadows.

"Hey, Dad."

He stopped and slowly turned back.

"Thanks."

He nodded.

I rubbed my nose with my glove. "You want to go somewhere and talk?"

He stared at me for the longest time. Then he said, "I'd like that."

I walked up to him. When we were an arm's length apart, we just looked at each other. Then a miracle happened. I reached out and hugged him. And at that moment the world I thought I knew no longer existed. At that moment, Stuart Smart became my father.

CHAPTER

Thirty

I do what I can to keep my mind here in Alabama. But my heart keeps wandering back to Utah.

✦ MARK SMART'S DIARY ✦

My dad and I probably talked more during the next two weeks than we did in our previous twenty-two years. I even volunteered to help him at the shop, and surprisingly it didn't feel like one of Dante's circles of Hell. One afternoon as we ate lunch together, I told him about Macy. He didn't say much, but I could tell he understood my pain. I also told him about Joette. I wondered how she was and if she'd told Macy how sick she really was. The thought of it made my stomach hurt.

"Are you going back?" My father asked.

I just shook my head. "I have no idea."

During my third week home I was working under a car when my dad crouched down next to me. "You have a visitor, son."

I rolled myself out on the creeper. Standing next to my dad was Tennys, my ex-girlfriend.

"Hey," she said.

I stood up, grabbing a rag from the

counter to wipe my hands. She looked even prettier than I remembered her, her long blond hair falling over one shoulder as if by accident. I knew Tennys well enough to know that nothing involving her looks was an accident. If I didn't know better, I would have thought she was trying to impress me.

"It's good to see you again, Mr. Smart," she said to my father.

"Pleasure seeing you again," my father said. He nodded to me, then left us alone.

"What's up?" I said.

"Hmm. Not much."

"That's hard to believe. Mrs. . . . ."

"No 'Mrs.' Unless you mean like 'misses the boat.' "

"You're not married yet?"

"We broke it off. No, actually *he* broke it off. His girlfriend came back."

"He had another girlfriend?"

"Long story."

"The cad," I said.

She smiled wryly. "I got a diamond out of it. I think he was just so embarrassed by it all that he told me to keep it." She looked at me, and there was a sweet vulnerability to her expression. "So how have you been?"

"I've survived."

"What's Salt Lake City like?"

"It's nice. Big mountains. Lots of snow. People are nice."

"Is school going well?"

"It was good while it lasted."

She rocked a little on the balls of her feet. "So how long are you back for?"

"I don't know. Maybe forever."

I could tell this pleased her. "Good. Well, I just wanted to welcome you home. I've got to get to work."

"Where are you working?"

"I got a job at Lord and Taylor's. I'm in the women's shoe department."

"You're doing what you love."

She laughed. "You've got me figured out, alright. With the employees' discount I spend most of my check before I get it." Her voice softened. "I was thinking that maybe after work we could get a coffee. Or dinner? I think it's my turn to buy."

I didn't answer.

"You can say no," she said. "Heaven knows I deserve it." She tilted her head a little. She knew it drove me crazy when she did that. "Just thought I'd ask."

She was being too humble to refuse. "What time do you get off?" I asked.

"Around six."

"I don't have a car. Unless I steal this one."

"I can pick you up."

"Okay. I'll see you then."

She smiled. "Can't wait."

C H A P T E R

Thirty-one

Tonight Tennys and I dined in vegetarian Hell. She made me an offer I'm not sure I should refuse.

✦ MARK SMART'S DIARY ✦

Tennys and I sat at a small table in the corner of Porky's Barbeque. Porky's was more than a restaurant—it was a temple to meat, where carnivore rituals were unabashedly practiced with a roll of paper towels at every table, an empty six-pack container filled with plastic squeeze bottles of barbecue sauce of varying heat and coleslaw and baked beans served by the pint.

I nixed Tennys's invitation to get coffee, as I hadn't eaten since lunch and, more important, I hadn't had any good barbeque since I left Alabama. I devoured a large platter of beef brisket and pork ribs while she daintily picked at a chicken breast and slaw.

Tennys looked beautiful, but then she always did. She was what my father called a "jaw-droppin' head-turner." She was wearing it well tonight.

"Are you living at home?" she asked when my mouth was full.

I nodded.

"With your father?" she asked, cringing a little.

"Things have changed," I said.

"Changed. Like Hell has frozen over?"

"I know. It's hard to believe."

"Well maybe it's true—absence does make the heart grow fonder."

"What does that say about together-ness?"

She thought about it. "I never really liked that saying."

I finished pulling the meat from a rib. "So tell me about the chiropractor."

"That's like asking Mrs. Lincoln how the play was."

"Sorry."

"It's okay. I probably should talk about it. I'm sure it's cathartic." She stopped her as-sault on the chicken. "I hurt my neck play-ing volleyball, so I went to that new chi-ropractor's office on Broadway for an adjustment. Boy, did I get one. I should have seen it coming. The first thing he asked is why such a pretty girl didn't have a ring. I didn't know that his girlfriend had dumped him the night before.

"The next thing I know, we're seeing each other every night. He's buying me chocolates, flowers, jewelry. I hadn't heard from you for a couple of weeks . . ."

"Don't blame this on me," I interjected, wiping sauce from my hands onto a paper towel. "This was all your doing?"

"Well, you *could* have called more," she said. "Anyway to my surprise he pops the question. And to my surprise I said yes."

"Just like that?"

"Swept away like a field mouse in a flash flood. It was kind of like ready, aim, fire. I said yes, then talked myself into it every day for the next three weeks. My mother was thrilled of course. She thought I had struck gold marrying a 'doctor.' She's running around making plans like it's her own wedding." Her expression changed. "But you know, I kept thinking about you. Of course, I was mad at you—that you hadn't asked me first. I even took some guilty pleasure writing you that Dear John. I found out the day after I sent it that your mother had died. I just felt sick. I wanted to call you. I called your dad for your number, but he told me he didn't have it. Then I was too embarrassed to go to the funeral. I didn't know what I'd say, and I thought I'd probably just make it harder for you. But I really was sorry. Your mother was a beautiful woman."

"I didn't go to the funeral," I said.

"What?"

"I wasn't in school. I lost my scholarship. But I didn't tell anyone, so when they tried to call me, they couldn't find me. I didn't find out until I called home two days after her funeral."

Tennys put her hand on mine. "I'm so sorry."

"Bad times," I said.

"I wish I could have been there for you."

"Me too," I said. I meant it.

After a moment she asked, "So did you leave a girlfriend in Salt Lake City?"

I wasn't sure that I wanted to tell her about Macy. "Sort of. She was really just a friend."

"Nothing serious then?"

I hesitated. "I asked her to marry me."

Her face registered surprise. "Really."

"Yes, I did."

"What did she say?"

"Nothing. She just kind of ran away."

Tennys looked at me for a moment, then started to laugh, softly at first, then obnoxiously loud. The people at the tables around us all looked to see what was so hilarious.

"It wasn't really that funny," I said.

She put her hand on my mine. "I'm sorry; I'm not laughing at you. The irony of it all is just delicious. Here we are, the heartthrobs of Roosevelt High, the king and queen of homecoming, and we're both dumped on the way to the altar. What a pair we make. We really are perfect for each other."

"You're right, it is pretty funny."

She sighed happily. "So maybe we should just run off together. I've already got the ring." She lifted her hand to show me. "Thank you, Dr. Ball."

"Wait, his last name is Ball?"

She nodded. "Uh-huh."

"Your name would have been Tennys Ball?"

She smiled. "I'm afraid so."

This time I burst out laughing. "It was doomed from the beginning."

She started laughing again. Then she leaned into me and we kissed. I knew from past experience that Tennys could kiss. The woman could have taught Rodin something. When we parted, I said, "You sure you want to marry a college dropout?"

"We'll have pretty babies."

I smiled. "Give me a day to think about it."

C H A P T E R

Thirty-two

My dad's a lot smarter than I've ever given him credit for. In truth I don't think he got a lot smarter—just I did.

I didn't get home until past two and woke to my radio-alarm clock less than four and a half hours later. I pulled on Levi's jeans and my crimson University of Utah sweatshirt and stumbled bleary-eyed into the kitchen. I took two waffles from the freezer and dropped them into the toaster as my dad watched in amusement, coffee in hand. "You was out late last night," he said.

"I was with Tennys."

He shook his head. "That girl is some kind of pretty. I thought she was getting herself hitched."

"She was. The guy called it off."

My father didn't say anything. He went to the refrigerator and brought out a package of salami, a head of lettuce and a jar of mayonnaise. "Salami sandwich okay?"

"Sure," I said, "But I can make it."

"I'm halfway there."

I slumped down at the table and closed my eyes. "Where's your Christmas tree?"

"With mother gone I just wasn't in the mood."

"It's not the same," I said.

"No," he said, "it ain't." My waffles popped up from the toaster and I got back up. I took the waffles and buttered them, then carried them back to the table.

"May I ask you something?"

He looked over at me, sensing the gravity of my question. "Maybe."

"Was Mom worth it?"

He didn't speak for a moment. "What do you mean?"

I carefully chose my words. "Now that I know the truth about everything . . . this marriage was really hard for you." I took a deep breath. "You're a good-looking guy, I'm sure there were other women . . ."

"There were a few."

"So what's so wrong with taking the easy road? Taking the sure thing."

He looked at me knowingly. "Tennys wants to marry you?"

I laughed. My father was smarter than I gave him credit for. "Yeah."

"Son, in matters of the heart there's no such thing as a sure thing." His brow furrowed. "I don't know that I've ever valued anything that came easy. Sometimes it's the fight that makes a thing worth having."

"And Mom was worth the fight?"

He looked at me seriously. "Every minute of it."

I let his words sink in. "The thing is, I don't know if she wants me. What if I go back just to get rejected again?"

My father looked at me thoughtfully. "Could happen. But you know what would be worse?"

"What?"

"If she was waiting for you, but you never went back because you was afraid."

I just stared at him. Then a smile slowly spread across my face. He dropped the sandwiches in a paper sack along with a half bag of barbeque potato chips. "You coming?"

"I think I have a plane to catch."

"Well, get on the phone with the airline. I can't be waiting for you all day."

CHAPTER
Thirty-three

*I called Tennys to tell her I was going
back to Utah. Though I think she was
disappointed, you wouldn't know it.
I swear you could tell that woman that
her hair was on fire and she'd ask if
the flames matched her blouse.*

✦ MARK SMART'S DIARY ✦

I left Huntsville three days before Christmas but didn't arrive in Salt Lake City until the day before Christmas Eve. In the mad rush of holiday travel, the airline had oversold the flight from Atlanta, and I was the only one willing to give up my seat for a free round-trip ticket, dinner and hotel stay. I called Victor from Alabama, and he agreed to pick me up from the airport and, somewhat begrudgingly, agreed to let me use the Malibu for the time I was in Utah.

The plane touched down in Salt Lake around seven at night. I found Victor reading a science fiction novel in the baggage claim area. I drove him home, then went straight to Macy's.

The duplex was dark, and three newspapers lay on the ground next to the front porch. Joette's car was still in the driveway, its windshield covered with an inch of snow, crusted hard with a layer of ice. Macy's car was gone. I rang the doorbell at least three times, but no one answered. Then I walked around the house and looked into the windows. There was no sign that anyone was there.

I puzzled over where to go next and decided on the Hut. It was a quiet night at the café. Christmas music was playing and there were a few couples sitting at tables, bags and boxes from last-minute shopping piled at their feet. I walked up to the front counter. The girl at the cash register recognized me.

"Hey, you're the guitar player."

"Yeah. Have you seen Macy?"

"Mary?"

"Whatever."

"Mary hasn't been on the schedule lately. I heard her mom's at the hospital. She was real sick."

My chest constricted. "Do you know which hospital?"

She shook her head. "Sorry, I wouldn't know."

"Who would?"

"I wouldn't know."

"She must have told someone. Maybe she wrote it down."

"Don't know if it'll do any good, but I'll

look in the back." She walked back to the office and returned a few minutes later. "I called Jeff. He said she's at Holy Cross Hospital."

"Thanks." I ran to the door.

"I hope you come back and play again," she shouted after me. "You were awesome."

⋆

I sped downtown to the hospital. I parked on the third level of the hospital's parking terrace and ran across the street. Christmas music played in the hospital's lobby. The volunteer at the reception desk wore a Santa hat and a jingle-bell necklace. She told me Joette was on the sixth floor of the hospital's west wing, Room 616.

It was a quarter past midnight when I walked into the semiprivate room. The two beds were separated by a drape hung between them from a metal rail.

Joette was asleep in the bed farthest from the door. The head of the bed was slightly raised and a small reading lamp was on above her. Macy was asleep next to her, her head resting against Joette's side. Even in the dim light I could see how much Joette had physically declined in the few weeks I was gone. If I hadn't known this was her room, I probably wouldn't have recognized her.

I had only been standing there a few minutes when a nurse walked in. I startled her. She said in a voice slightly above a whisper, "It's past visiting hours. You'll have to leave."

I gestured for the nurse to follow me, and we stepped out into the hallway. "I'm sorry. I just got in town. How is she?"

She frowned. "She's dying. Her liver is shutting down."

"How long does she have?"

"I don't know. I've seen people in her condition last a few hours and I've seen them linger on for days. It's all in God's time. But I don't expect it will be too much longer." She frowned. "I'm sorry, but unless you're immediate family, visiting hours were over at nine."

"The thing is she asked me to look after her daughter. And if this is her last night, I should be here."

The nurse looked at me for a moment, unsure of what to do.

"It's Christmas," I said, playing the holiday trump card.

"Alright."

"Thank you."

The nurse returned to her rounds and I went back inside the room. There was a recliner next to Joette's bed and I sat back in it. I mostly watched Macy as she lay sleeping next to her mother. I wondered how long she'd gone without sleep. I wanted to hold her and comfort her just as she had me the night we first met. She moaned lightly in her sleep. I walked over to her side and put my arm around her. She shifted a little, said something I didn't understand, then raised her head and looked around, her eyes droopy, her hair matted to one side. She looked at me, blinked several times, then her eyes widened. She said in a whisper, "Mark?"

"Hi, Mace."

She stared at me in disbelief. "You came back."

"I did."

"Joette . . ."

"I know," I said. I pulled her into me and held her. Then I said, "Come here."

I helped her up from the chair, then led

her back to the recliner, sat down and pulled her onto my lap. She cuddled into me. Then she lifted her head. "What exactly are you doing here, Mr. Smart?"

"Just rest," I said. "Get your sleep. I'll watch Joette."

She laid her head back into my chest. "You came back," she said sleepily.

I put my hand on the back of her head and gently stroked her hair. "Yeah," I said, "I'm back."

CHAPTER
Thirty-four

I have come to believe that there are moments too profound to be contained in time.

✦ MARK SMART'S DIARY ✦

CHRISTMAS EVE

I woke early the next morning with Macy still asleep in my arms. Joette was awake and looking at us. In the predawn morning light I could see the jaundiced tint of her skin and eyes. Still, she looked peaceful.

"Hi, Joette," I said softly.

"Hi, Mark."

I reached for her hand. It felt small and fragile in mine. "How are you?" I asked. In the history of stupid questions this had to be the atom bomb of them all.

She forced a smile. I gently rubbed my thumb across her hand. "I'm sorry."

"Me too," she whispered.

She closed her eyes and appeared to fall back asleep. Twenty minutes later she opened her eyes again. Her speech was slurred but coherent. "Did you see your father?"

I nodded. "Yes. All is well in Oz."

She smiled.

"Thank you, Joette. You've done so much for Macy. And for me."

She ran her tongue over her teeth. "Take care of my girl."

"I will."

She closed her eyes again and fell back to sleep. Macy also continued to sleep. Around eight a nurse came in and checked Joette's vitals. She didn't say anything to me but didn't need to. Joette's final journey had begun.

Macy woke shortly after nine. She jerked upright, afraid that Joette might have slipped away while she slept. I guessed her thoughts and squeezed her hand. "She's still here," I said.

Again, Macy seemed surprised to see me, and I suspect that earlier she may have thought my return a dream. Macy got up and used the restroom, then returned to her vigil in the plastic chair next to Joette's bed. I went down to the cafeteria and got Macy an orange juice and a bagel with cream cheese, neither of which she ever touched.

The next eighteen hours crawled by. Joette slept, waking a few times to look for Macy. Macy periodically rubbed Vaseline on

Joette's parched lips and moistened her mouth with oral swabs. Through it all Macy never left her side.

After midnight the nurse on call began upping Joette's dose of morphine, and she became less coherent and less aware of her surroundings. At one point Joette looked up to a corner of the room and just stared. Then a tear fell down her cheek and she spoke in a clear voice: "Not yet."

"Do you see someone?" Macy asked.

Her voice was a whisper. "Angel."

"You see an angel?" I asked.

"No," Macy said. She leaned close to Joette's cheek. "Is Angela here?"

Joette silently mouthed a yes.

Macy's eyes filled with tears. "Go with her, Mom. You can leave. I'll be okay."

Joette turned and looked into Macy's eyes.

Macy began sobbing softly. "I love you."

After a few minutes I came over and put my hand on Macy's back. Then I leaned over and kissed Joette on the forehead. "Merry Christmas, Jo," I said softly. "To you and Angela."

I don't know exactly how long we sat

there that Christmas Eve, in the dim little room on the sixth floor of Holy Cross Hospital, but somewhere in the night, for the second time in her life, Macy lost her mother.

CHAPTER

Thirty-five

The world is a little darker today.

✦ MARK SMART'S DIARY ✦

JOETTE'S FUNERAL

Joette was buried two days after Christmas. I offered Macy some of the money my father had given me to pay for her service, but she didn't need it. Joette had already made all the arrangements and paid the funeral home in advance. Even in death she was looking after Macy.

The service was beautiful. It was held at a nearby Mormon church, and the burial was at a small suburban cemetery called Elysian Fields.

There were more than a hundred people at Joette's service, most of them former Denny's employees and her customers. It was an eclectic bunch. Some wore traditional suits or dresses, but there were also those in Harley-Davidson leathers, old men with tweed slacks and cardigan sweaters and truck drivers in denim and flannel. Joette belonged to all of them. She was waitress, marriage counselor, therapist and for a few of them, dream girl. One gruff-looking truck driver who wore broad-lens aviator glasses to hide his grief left a ten-dollar bill on her casket. I guess he wanted to leave her one last tip.

After the funeral we were stopped on the way to our car by a man who introduced himself as Joette's ex–brother-in-law. With-out an explanation, he handed Macy a manila envelope, expressed his condo-lences, then walked away.

I drove Macy back to her house. I knew that going home without Joette would be especially difficult, and I was right: Macy nearly collapsed as we walked inside. I car-ried her to the couch and I held her as she wept. Her grief was inconsolable.

We sat there in the soft glow of the Christ-mas tree lights, grieving the loss of a friend. The only thing Macy said was, "This was meant to happen at Christmas. That's the way Jo would have wanted it."

It was several hours later before Macy opened the envelope. Inside was a copy of Joette's will. Not surprisingly, Joette had been planning her departure for some time. She had saved a decent nest egg and purchased a small insurance policy that paid off the mortgage on the duplex. Not surprisingly, she had left everything to Macy.

There was also another envelope containing a letter that had been written during Joette's final weeks. Macy opened the envelope and unfolded the linen stationery. The paper was embossed with two ruby slippers set above the words *There's no place like home.* Just seeing Joette's handwriting caused Macy to cry. In between her tears she slowly read the letter.

> *To my Sweet Macy,*
> *When you receive this letter, I will be gone. But not forever. One night, as I struggled in the midnight hours with my pain and fear, I prayed with all the energy of my heart to know what awaited me on the other side. God spoke to my soul, and I knew for a certainty that all would be well—that I would not only be reunited with my Angela but, someday, with you as well. From that moment on I've felt at peace. I know your heart is breaking right now, but fear not. God has conquered death. And one day we will*

all be home again. Together. I'll be waiting for you, my darling. But in the meantime make the most of every moment you are blessed to have. Love. Hurt. Laugh. Cry. Dance. Stumble. And drink lots of chocolate!!!

There's one more thing I wanted you to know. I have always looked forward to the day when you had a child of your own. It is one of the greatest disappointments of my life that I won't get to share that with you. Let me tell you now—you WILL feel inadequate. You will wonder how you can do it right, especially since you never really had a good role model of your own. But don't worry, you'll do fine. Any child would be lucky to have you as a mother. Remember, in the end what really matters is that you love. You'll make mistakes every day, but somehow love just washes them away like a wave cleansing the beach, and each day you start anew.

My sweet Macy, your heart abounds in love! I know, because I've been the lucky recipient of it for these wonderful years we've shared. I have been the luckiest of women. You were God's gift to me. I have grown to respect and revere you in so many ways. I once told a customer that I wanted to grow up and be like you. Thank you for teaching me what it means to be a friend. All I've ever given you was a small portion back of what you've given me. I'll be waiting. But don't come too soon. You still have a lot of life to live! Eternally yours,

Your mother,
Jo

C H A P T E R

Thirty-six

I am grateful for new years and new beginnings. It is a great human need to be periodically reborn.

✦ MARK SMART'S DIARY ✦

NEW YEAR'S EVE

The living room fireplace crackled and hissed as Macy and I sat together on the couch watching Dick Clark and the crowds in Times Square. It was not even ten o'clock when Macy asked to turn off the television. She wasn't in the mood for festivities, televised or otherwise. I had made us dinner—barbequed ribs, my mother's recipe—and we had eaten in the living room. Macy took our plates back into the kitchen and began filling the sink with water, when the doorbell rang.

"Are you expecting someone?" I asked.

"No."

I went to the door and opened it. A young woman stood in the doorway. She looked like she had stepped from the window of an exclusive Park City boutique and wore a beautiful full-length shearling coat. Even though I had never seen her before, I had no doubt who I was looking at, for she looked just like Macy. It was Noel.

"I'm looking for Macy Wood," she said. "Is my sister here?"

"We've been looking for you."

"I know."

"Come on in."

Noel stepped inside. "Hey, Macy," I called. Just then Macy walked back into the living room. "Who was—" she froze. For a minute the two women just stared at each other, unsure of how to react.

Noel spoke first. "Hi, Macy."

"Noel."

Noel walked to her and a big smile crossed her face. Then they threw their arms around each other. "I can't believe it," Macy said. "I can't believe it."

"Why don't you sit down," I said. What else was there to say?

The two sisters sat next to each other, their eyes fixed on each other's faces.

"I didn't think your mother would tell you about me," Macy said.

"She wasn't going to. I made her tell me."

"But how did you know to ask?"

"I found this." She pulled a yellowed piece of paper from her coat pocket and handed it to Macy. "It's a letter from Mom. Our mom."

Macy read:

My little Noel,
It's two in the morning, and for the past several hours I've been lying here staring at the clock, unable to sleep. I do not sleep well these days. The cancer makes it hard to find any comfort. My body is weakening, but my mind is full of energy, so I need to write while I still can. I worry constantly about what will happen when I am gone. Your father has struggled with his addiction. He has been good of late, but I worry what will happen without me. Oh, how I hope I'm wrong. I made him promise, for your sakes, that he will beat this. For if he fails, I don't know what will become of you. This fear grips my heart even more than death. Who will take care of my babies? Your big sister, Macy, seems to sense this. She's only five, yet she watches over you like a mother hen. I know she'll try her best to take care of you. She

already does. I worry for her, because the world is too big, too hard, for a little girl. If Dad doesn't keep his promise, you will be taken away from him, and it is possible that you could be separated from each other. I pray that this is not the case. You are still so small, you might not even remember your sister. I write this note, like a note in a bottle, sent with hope that providence might lead you to it. I know that someday, when the time is right, you will find this. When you do, you must find your sister. You must be together. I don't know what influence I might have from the other realm, but I will do what I can. Wherever you are, my love, know that I am looking over you and your sister. I love you with all my heart.

Mom

Macy looked back up at Noel.

"Where did you get this?"

"I was helping my mom put away the Christmas ornaments when one of them— my special ornament—fell from the tree and shattered. At first I was heartbroken. Then I saw this note in the middle of the broken glass."

She took Macy's hand. "When I read it, it was as if a dam broke. All these memories just poured into my head. And suddenly everything made sense—why I don't look a thing like my brothers or my parents." She put her hand on Macy's knee. "But more than that, I finally understood the dreams. I've dreamt about a girl named Macy my whole life. She was my imaginary friend. Whenever I was sad or afraid, she was there for me.

"Once, when I was seven, I was walking home from school when the neighbor boys started teasing me. One of them stole my lunchbox, and I suddenly shouted out for you. I had no idea why. I just shouted 'Macy.' They looked around, and then they dropped my lunchbox and ran away. I didn't know why I had said your name. But from then on I believed that if I said it I'd be safe." She looked at Macy and smiled. "Thank you for always being there for me."

Macy's eyes filled with tears. "Do you think Mom had something to do with the ornament breaking?"

Noel smiled. "I'm sure of it."

Macy suddenly stood and walked over to the Christmas tree, where her own ornament hung. She carefully lifted the hook from its bough and delicately held up the bauble, her face reflecting in its crimson sheen. "My mother was with me all along." She turned and looked back at us. "I've protected this my whole life."

"Maybe it's finally time to break it," I said.

Noel looked over at me. "I'm sorry, I didn't ask. Are you Macy's husband?"

Macy looked at me and for a moment neither of us spoke. Then she said softly, "If he'll still have me."

A broad smile crossed my face. "You have great timing, Noel. You arrived just in time to see your big sister get engaged."

*I've come to know that our families
are a canvas on which we paint our
greatest hopes—imperfect and sloppy,
for we are all amateurs at life, but if we
do not focus too much on our mistakes,
a miraculous picture emerges. And we
learn that it's not the beauty of the
image that warrants our gratitude—it's
the chance to paint.*

✶ MARK SMART'S DIARY ✶

Macy and I were married the next year on November 3, the anniversary of when we first met. Instead of a wedding cake, we served a tower of death-by-chocolate brownies from the Hut. It just seemed right somehow.

My father flew out for the wedding. It was

his first time on an airplane. The flight wasn't as bad as he feared, and he even enjoyed the in-flight meal. My father has simple tastes.

Macy's father also attended the ceremony, but he didn't give her away. Macy didn't like the idea of him doing that again. He died just three months later of cirrhosis of the liver. Macy and Noel were both at his side when he passed. I'm not really sure how much his death affected Macy, but it was nothing like Joette's. *Law of the harvest,* I guess; you reap what you sow.

※

Noel was Macy's maid of honor. Even now I'm amazed at how similar the two women are—not just in looks but in mannerisms and thought. You'd think they'd never been apart. They're inseparable now, and I joke that if I'd known how much time they'd be spending with each other I never would have helped facilitate their reunion. I guess they're just making up for lost time.

Tennys got married just three months after I left, to a young medical resident in

Birmingham. She finally got her doctor. I'm sure she has pretty babies.

✦

It's been fifteen Christmases since I met Macy, and I love her more now than I ever knew was possible. That's not to say we don't have our problems. Everyone brings baggage into a relationship and the two of us have more than our share. But that's just life. I once read that love is like a rose: we fixate on the blossom, but it's the thorny stem that keeps it alive and aloft. I think marriage is like that. Like my father said, the things of greatest value are the things we fight for. And in the end, if we do it right, we value the stem far more than the blossom.

Shortly after we were married, I used my school money to open my first guitar shop and school: Smart Guitars. Since then we've opened three more stores. We currently have more than two hundred students. I've never heard a song I wrote played on the radio, but it's just as well. I only write them for Macy and she likes to keep them for herself.

Macy and I have three children of our

own. A boy and two girls. Sam, Alice and Jo. I wonder what kind of parent I am. I do my best. Sometimes I suppose I even get it right. Kids don't come with owner's manuals. You have to figure each of them out, and by the time you do, they're gone. I pray that I didn't do them too much harm, and hope, for their sakes, that they will forgive me someday as well.

My father is getting old now and men get soft and sentimental with age. He sold the garage a few years back, and now spends his time puttering around the house. He discovered the Internet and keeps a Web site posted with pictures of his grandchildren. I see him at least once a year; with each visit he seems less able and less well. I don't know how much longer he'll be around, but I'm grateful that he still is. We invited him to live with us, but he declined. It's not home.

I was afraid of how Macy would view Christmas after losing Joette on that day, but my fear was unjustified. The day only became more holy to her, as it was the day Joette was reunited with her little angel. Every Christmas Eve we light two candles, one for Joette and one for Angela. Macy places them close together so their flames become one.

There are stories, Christmas stories that are stored away like boxes of garlands and frosted glass ornaments, to be brought out and cherished each year. I've come to believe that my story is a Christmas story. For it has forever changed the way I see Christmas.

That season I learned perspective, for Joseph the carpenter and Stuart the auto mechanic both raised someone else's son. We don't know much about Joseph; the Bible tells us little. But I've gained a new respect for the man.

Just like our story, the original Christmas tales were stories of searching, not so much for the lost, as for the familiar. Mary and Joseph sought in Bethlehem—the home of their familial ancestry—a place to start their own family; the three kings from the East journeyed beneath that sentinel star to find the King of Kings; and the shepherds sought a child in a place most familiar to them: a manger.

And perhaps after all the songs and poems and stories of the season, Christmas is really no more than that—humanity's search for the familiar. Every year we bring out the same songs, partake of the same foods and traditions, and share the things that make us feel that there's someplace we belong. And in the end all any of us are looking for is home.

Richard Paul Evans is the author of ten *New York Times* best-selling novels and five children's books. He has won the American Mothers' Book Award, the *Romantic Times* 2005 Best Women's Fiction award and two first-place Storytelling World Awards for his children's books. His books have been translated into more than eighteen languages. More than 13 million copies of his books are in print worldwide. Evans is also the founder of the Christmas Box House International, an organization dedicated to helping abused and neglected children. More than 13,000 children have been housed in Christmas Box Houses. He is the recipient of the *Washington Times* Humanitarian of the Century Award and the Volunteers of America Empathy Award. He lives in Salt Lake City, Utah, with his wife and five children.

Visit Richard Paul Evan's Web site and join his e-mail list for free reading group discussion guides, book and tour updates, and special offers:

www.richardpaulevans.com

Please send written correspondence to

Richard Paul Evans
P.O. Box 1416
Salt Lake City, Utah 84110